ODYSSEUS

ODYSSEUS

A Life

CHARLES ROWAN BEYE

AN IMPRINT OF HYPERION
NEW YORK

Library of Congress Cataloging-in-Publication Data

Beye, Charles Rowan.
  Odysseus : a life / Charles Rowan Beye.—1st ed.
    p. cm.
  ISBN 1-4013-0024-3
    1. Odysseus (Greek mythology)—Fiction. 2. Trojan War—
Fiction. I. Title.

PS3602.E93O34 2004
813'.6—dc21

                                                            2003049967

Hyperion books are available for special promotions and premiums.
For details contact Michael Rentas, Manager, Inventory and Pre-
mium Sales, Hyperion, 77 West 66th Street, 11th floor, New York,
New York 10023-6298, or call 212-456-0133.

FIRST EDITION

10 9 8 7 6 5 4 3 2

For Richard Deppe

ACKNOWLEDGMENTS

Bob Miller gave me the idea for this book. Mark Chait was my superlative editor. I might not have proceeded except for the encouragement of Deborah Greenman. Richard Deppe helped me with the research, Ann Rosener gave the completed text its first very critical read, and Mary DeForest showered me with her brilliant suggestions. I have had many rewarding, if spirited, conversations with Sebastian Lockwood, whose years of performing the *Odyssey* story has made Odysseus as real to him as any companion, and as dear as his best friend. I thank them all—particularly Richard, who was good enough to listen to me talk of Odysseus as though he were our houseguest for months on end.

CONTENTS

PREFACE

Somehow everyone seems to know something about Odysseus, how he wandered the Mediterranean seas for ten years trying to get home, or how he killed the Cyclops, or killed the suitors who were swarming around his wife, Penelope, back at the palace in Ithaca. Or Penelope, for that matter, faithful Penelope. Or Telemachus, the insubstantial young son, yearning for his hero father. These are staples of the western imagination.

Odysseus turns up century after century. He's the main character in the *Odyssey*, of course, and plays a major role in the *Iliad*. Both are poetic narratives, oral poems. Although their authorship is entirely unknown, they are said to be the works of a certain Homer, a convenient handle for scholars, librarians, and anyone else who needs to categorize texts. In any case these two stories passed from mouth to ear, were stored in the memory and brain, for hundreds of years before they were ever written down. Who knows the vast number of lost narratives in which Odysseus may have figured? By the fifth century B.C.E., when the Athenian dramatist Sophocles put him into two plays, *Ajax* and *Philoctetes*, he was a familiar feature of the culture, much more substantial and ubiquitous in the community imagination than most fictional characters, more like a figure from history.

Although Odysseus' advanced capacity for mendacity made them nervous, the Romans adopted him, like everything else Greek, giving him the name Ulixes, which is how they learned to pronounce "Odysseus" from the Etruscans, and that is the name, in the spelling Ulysses, with which he has come down in the western literary tradition. The Italian Renaissance took him up, even though not always ready to heap praise; Dante disapproved, but then Odysseus as a pagan Greek scarcely had a chance with that severely legalistic Christian Florentine. In Victorian England, Tennyson reminded his comfortable bourgeois audience of the heroism of Odysseus' eternal questing. James Joyce rather loosely plotted Leopold Bloom's walk through Dublin on Odysseus and his wandering. Bloom, a Jew in Catholic Dublin, was Joyce's shrewd reference to the essential alienation of his ancient model. The trials and wonders of Odysseus' ten-year voyage gave the twentieth-century Alexandrian Greek Constantine Cavafy the inspiration for one of his greatest pieces, "Ithaca," a poem about how the life lived, the journey taken, matters far more than the end, the home port of Ithaca. Americans will remember that "Ithaca" was read at the funeral service of Jacqueline Kennedy Onassis.

If the truth is that Odysseus is essentially a narrative device, a verbal construct, a fiction, an anthropological phenomenon (i.e., "the trickster figure"), an embodiment of action, it is nonetheless challenging to conceive the character whole. A totem as familiar as this Homeric figure who exercises the imagination over the millennia from culture to culture deserves a biography in which the many-faceted artifice we call Odysseus is given a life set out from a beginning to an end. Beginning to end begets cause and effect, and in this way action, the essence of ancient narrative, is made to yield up its implications.

NAMES

The unsuspecting reader who comes to this account of Odysseus may feel drowned in the luxuriant stew of names, sometimes two names for the same thing. It is the heritage of the thousands of years gone by, during which everything has been thought and rethought. Odysseus is considered a **Bronze Age** figure. That term defines a time when tools and other metal objects were still made of bronze, followed obviously enough by the so-called **Iron Age**, when that stronger and more durable metal had supplanted bronze in the fabrication of most utensils. One can also say that Odysseus grew up at the close of the **second millennium B.C.** or, as it is more neutrally rendered nowadays, **second millennium B.C.E.**, that is to say "before the Common Era." Others call Odysseus a product of the **Heroic Age**, a term that originally comes from the fact that in the earliest accounts written in the Greek language men of the aristocratic warrior class are sometimes designated by the Greek word *heros*. The English word "hero," which derives from *heros*, has a lot of romantic nonsense invested into it, coming by way of the European Middle Ages and chivalric codes when men kept themselves in a state of spiritual readiness and fought battles that were called Crusades, despite their economic and political undertones. All this was inherited by nineteenth-century romanticism, which willy-nilly rubs off on contemporary conceptions of these ancient Greek figures. In using one of these three terms—Bronze Age, Heroic Age, or second millennium—the choice probably says a lot about the person making it.

The area in which Odysseus grew to adulthood is known today as **Greece**, the people among whom Odysseus lived are commonly called **Greeks**, and their language is also known to linguists as **Greek**. The words "Greek" and "Greece" were invented by the Romans, along with so much else bequeathed to the western world, but not much liked by the people so named. They prefer **Hellenes**, and **Hellenic** for the language, but neither was in use in Odysseus' time. Rather his people were called **Achaeans**, the land **Achaea**. Sometimes, however, the language is called **Mycenaean** and the people **Mycenaeans** because the center of power in the second millennium seems to have been located at **Mycenae**, a rocky citadel south of present-day Corinth and slightly northwest of modern Nauplion. Mycenae's legendary ruler, **Agamemnon**, exercised some kind of nominal control over all the other local aristocrats, lords, and chiefs scattered in small settlements throughout the mainland and the islands of the Aegean and Ionian Seas.

The Greek language is one of what is called the Indo-European family of languages. At the end of the third millennium B.C.E., mass movements of people speaking some kind of Indo-European precursor of Greek came down through the present-day Balkans and spread out over the mainland to the south and the islands to the east and the west. Their dialect of Indo-European evolved into a separate language, which linguists call Greek. They established an empire and engaged in trade with their neighbors throughout the Mediterranean. As trade tends to go hand in hand with warfare, we read a lot about plunder, and there are accounts of these people as hostile forces in several areas. Around the end of the second millennium B.C.E., the Mycenaeans clashed with a large and powerful culture whose center, the ancient citadel called **Troy**, was located at the entrance to the Dardanelles (it is near the modern Turkish city Hissarlik). It so happens that the makers of the oral poetic tradition in the early period of Greek culture settled on that venue for the narrative of one of the great battle stories of all time. The truth or falsehood of the account is not verifiable and doesn't really matter. There are some things that are true in another way, and the Trojan War is one of them.

The story of the Trojan War was treated as history by the ancients, and, because it has been around for so long and told in so many different ways to so many different audiences, it has become an honorary fact, so to speak, for the whole of the western world. There are, in fact, many persons in the last two centuries who considered it a truth, one of them the wealthy nineteenth-century businessman Heinrich Schliemann, who spent a fortune on archeological digs and found abundant evidence of civilization both at Hissarlik and Mycenae, which he promptly declared were the sites described in the poems the *Iliad* and the *Odyssey*. Odysseus' life is partly defined by his role in the Trojan War; not only does this legitimate a kind of historical existence for him, but that association has also given a kind of veracity to his subsequent ordeal of return to his native land, a series of adventures that frequently border on the miraculous. Odysseus has the kind of character of which much could be posited, and the ancients took his initial story and embroidered upon it, so that the

Odysseus figure became far more complicated and three-dimensional than the usual literary construct that exists solely in one text. The explosion of information in the twentieth century, together with the privileging of the scientific method, has tended to overshadow and sometimes extinguish legend masquerading as history. This is a pity. As Aristotle once observed, legend is truer than history, since it presents what human psychology needs to know is true, whereas history is only a succession of events that have happened. The struggle of Odysseus to get home and, once there, to destroy the men who were besieging his wife can be read in infinitely different ways. Historical fact does not usually have that depth.

Here are the basics (a Glossary appears at the end of the book): Odysseus was the son of King **Laertes** and Queen **Anticleia**. He grew up with his sister, **Ctimene**, in the palace. Among their many attendants were the nanny **Eurycleia** and the swineherd **Eumaeus**, who stand out for their loyalty; and the goatherd **Melanthius** and the table waitress and kitchen helper **Melantho**, both of whom seem to be rotten apples. King Laertes ruled the island of **Ithaca** and adjacent lands, all part of the nominal domain of the king of Mycenae, **Agamemnon**. Agamemnon was married to **Clytemnestra**. His brother, **Menelaus**, king of **Sparta**, was married to her sister, the fabulous **Helen**, who ran off with a prince from Troy named **Paris**, a provocation that caused Agamemnon to declare war on Troy and demand fleets and troops from his subjects. Odysseus was married to the cousin of these two sisters, **Penelope**, by whom he had one son, **Telemachus.** Shortly thereafter, he went off to fight at Troy with a contingent of local men. The war was a bitter, seemingly endless affair of ten long years, in which Odysseus probably got to know better than he wanted to the arrogant Agamemnon, the wimpy Menelaus, the tiresome old **Nestor**, the self-obsessed **Achilles**, his son **Neoptolemus**, the two prima donnas **Ajax** and **Philoctetes,** as well as a lot of great guys whom anyone would hope to find fighting next to him in a risky situation, like his favorite battle companion, **Diomedes**. Helen languished the war away inside the walls of Troy with, among others, her always beautiful, sexy consort Paris; his serious, dutiful brother, **Hector**; and the old king, **Priam**, and his queen, **Hecuba**.

After the war ended with the destruction of Troy, Odysseus sailed for home, but rounding **Cape Malea** was blown off his course for ten more years. His second in command was his sister's brother-in-law, **Eurylochus**, who brought him nothing but grief. During this time, Odysseus was hounded by the god of the sea, **Poseidon**, who wanted to avenge Odysseus' cruel treatment of his son, but he was also helped by the goddess **Athena**, who for reasons of her own had an enduring affection for him. On his gale-blown wanderings he encountered a wide variety of people from what seems the land of fairy tale: the friendly **Lotus-eaters**; Poseidon's son, the giant **Cyclops**, who ate some of the crew for dinner; King **Aeolus**, who gave him favoring winds; the giant hostile **Laestrygonians**; the witch **Circe** on the island of **Aiaia**, who turned men into swine but kept Odysseus for herself in bed; the seer **Tiresias**, whom Odysseus went to meet in the **Underworld**; the **Sirens** whose sweet singing drove men mad; the giant water monsters **Scylla** and **Charybdis**, who nearly drowned him; the sea nymph **Calypso** on whose island, **Ogygia**, Odysseus was washed up when **Zeus** had destroyed his entire fleet and crew with a thunderbolt for having eaten the cattle of **Helios**, as the sun god was known in Greece; and the **Phaeaceans** on the island of **Scheria**, whose king, **Alcinous**, and queen, **Arete**, at last provided a ship to send the weary fellow home, despite the obvious desire of their beautiful sixteen-year-old daughter, **Nausicaa**, that he stay and become her husband.

Back to Ithaca he went. At home his wife, Penelope, was sur-rounded by all the younger men of the territory who wanted her to declare Odysseus dead, herself a widow, and nominate one of them to succeed to the throne. The three leaders were **Eurymachus, Antinous,** and **Amphinomus**. With the active help of Athena, who more or less plays Fairy Godmother to his Cinderella, Odysseus insinuates himself among the suitors at the palace in the disguise of a beggar. There ensues a tension-filled series of moves until, with a lot of help from Athena, and vital assistance from his son, Telemachus, the swineherd Eumaeus, and the oxherd **Philoitius**, the suitors are killed and Odysseus is reunited with Penelope.

ODYSSEUS

CHAPTER 1

•◆•

PRINCE

O<small>DYSSEUS IS THE</small> perpetual enigma who tells all and reveals nothing. "The man of many turns," they called him, twisting and turning himself, always coming up with another answer, eluding everyone's grasp, like a fish from the sea, or a snake caught in the grass. Or like Proteus, the old sea sprite who would never give up his secrets but writhed, changed shape, size, aspect until his would-be interlocutors managed to pin him to the ground and he ceased his rapid permutations. The protean man, that is Odysseus: he is the father crying in the embrace of his son; the son coldly deceiving and testing his father; the husband spurning an amorous nymph's gift of immortality to return to the bed of his wife; the lusty lover whose comrades must force him from yet another woman's bed; the man pretending insanity to escape his military obligation; the wise military leader and the soldier of exceptional strength and valor; the liar, as some would call him; the storyteller, the maker of fictions, his admirers say; athlete, sailor, navigator, shipbuilder; hated by many, respected by most; doubted, suspected, not exactly liked except by women. But then being liked was not one of the concerns of a prince of the Greek Bronze Age.

Odysseus is a product of this Bronze Age. His father, Laertes, was the ruler of Ithaca, and Odysseus grew up to succeed him. Ithaca is an island twenty miles off the western coast of northern Greece; it is separated by a narrow channel from the island of Cephalonia, which sits out in the Ionian Sea at the entrance to the Gulf of Patras. On a ship sailing from Patras to Corfu or on to Brindisi while coming out of the Gulf of Patras, the modern traveler might notice "the impressive bold and barren outline of the mountains and cliffs," as the *Blue Guide* describes Ithaca. Seventeen miles long, four miles wide, second smallest of the Ionian Islands, it is nothing more than two peninsulas of rugged hills separated by a low-lying isthmus, "no wide spaces to keep horses, no meadows, only steep slopes, a place for goats," as Odysseus' son, Telemachus, was to describe it. Here and there, a pocket-sized valley had soil enough for olives or almond trees, and the upper slopes held cultivated vines. In the springtime, wild flowers sprang up among the oleander, myrtle, and cypress trees. Wild thyme perfumed the air, a source of pollen for bees, who endowed their honey with its special scent. Small, inconsequential, Ithaca might scarcely be noticed by the modern traveler before it vanishes from view. Few persons in the ancient world would have ever visited there. Ithaca was a long way from Mycenae, the center of power in the second millennium. Odysseus' son, Telemachus, on his first visit to the mainland, acted like the country rube he was, scarcely knowing how to grace a banquet table on his visit to old Nestor in Pylos, and then in Sparta moving in absolute awe through the grand halls of Menelaus' palace. It is pretty clear that Ithaca was really the boondocks.

Still Laertes was the king, for what the title is worth, on this small island. Despite its minuscule size, Ithaca was the seat of a power that encompassed several of the neighboring islands. We know this because when the expedition was raised to fight against the Trojans, Odysseus is listed as the acknowledged leader of the contingent, which included men from such nearby islands as Cephalonia and Zacynthus, as well as from part of the mainland. These were the territories from which, fifteen years later, the younger sons, the ones left behind when the ships had sailed, came to Ithaca, like ants when honey is spilled, to woo Odysseus' wife, Penelope, when it began to seem like a reasonable gamble that Odysseus would die or had died at Troy. However beautiful Penelope may have been, it wasn't sexual attraction that drew them to the palace, it was the royal succession.

The local leader may have been called "king," but he did not behave like the European royals of the last millennium, whose model for behavior was the Roman emperor and his successors. The second millennium B.C.E. was a simpler time. Compared with the design of European palaces, Mycenaean palace architecture was definitely modest, even if the rooms for public access had a certain grandeur to them. On the small and remote island of Ithaca, Laertes' palace must have been a very simple affair. Everything centered on the throne room, a space that measured something like fifty feet by thirty feet; the most important public room of the complex, it was reached through a grand stone entrance porch. What marked the space was a stone seat along one wall larger than any others; this was for the king. In the center of the room was a great circular hearth, surrounded by four columns that supported the roof beams as well as the raised clerestory walls above it from which the smoke of the fire escaped. Whatever heat there was in these stone structures came from this hearth, which was also the site of libations, sacrifice, and prayers to the ever constant, ever present divinities. In his childhood Odysseus was encouraged to sense the presence of gods at this hearth. Fire is a fine expression of the mystery of existence; who can ever tire of gazing at it? Odysseus—whose adult life was spent first in the flickering uncertainties of warfare, then as a castaway at sea—never lost his feeling for the intimations of a divine presence that surrounded him, inhabited the spaces through which he walked or sailed, thrust him onward or pulled him back on his journey through life.

The other public rooms were also on the ground floor: the dining hall, the pantry storerooms for crockery, the kitchens, and washrooms, as well as sleeping areas for travelers and the resident males. The women were lodged above the ground floor, where the children also stayed. Odysseus' son, Telemachus, once he was no longer a child, had left the women's quarters to stay in a small, separate building nearby, a bedroom to which one of the slave women lighted his way at night. When Odysseus married, he had designed and built a nuptial suite, but because it was on the ground floor, the prudent Penelope had left it once the suitors filled the throne room and the dining room night after night. Staying on the ground floor was compromising, if not downright dangerous. In Mycenaean palaces, the women's area was upstairs for the very good reason that the women needed protection against the often ruthless behavior of males. Penelope naturally moved upstairs, where the other women stayed, not long after Odysseus had departed for the war. She could still present herself from time to time downstairs in the company of her personal attendants, as indeed we have record of her doing.

Powerful women surrounded Odysseus throughout his life, as is clear from the account of his travels after the war. He already had the example in his mother, Anticleia. She figures in a marvelous story about her husband's slave, Eurycleia, whom Laertes had bought for himself when she was a young girl. This enslaved woman must have been good-looking since he was said to have paid well for her, that is, twenty head of cattle. The strange thing is that he never once got into bed with her—something that would have been expected and normal in any slave master—even though "he favored her," so it is said, "as much as his wife." And why? "He wanted to steer clear of his wife's anger," they said. Laertes was either a wimp in patriarch's clothing or he understood all too well the value of Anticleia. Maybe he was in love with her—that would explain his extreme change in behavior when she died. But "wife's anger" might also be just gossip. One could argue that Laertes knew from the start what an intelligent and stalwart addition to the household Eurycleia would be. As is clear from the evidence, she would remain a powerful aid to the family long after she ceased to serve as nursemaid to Odysseus and, later, to his son, Telemachus.

Compare this story with Agamemnon's attitude toward domestic chastity. He publicly declared before the Achaean army at Troy that the newly arrived slave girl Chryseis suited him just fine, good if not better than his wife, Clytemnestra, and he intended to take her home to Mycenae with him; then after the war had ended and he was given the virgin priestess, the Trojan Cassandra, to be his sexual slave as part of his plunder, he returned to his palace in Mycenae with Princess Cassandra in tow and, in front of the assembled townspeople, handed her over to Clytemnestra to set up in the women's quarters. There is a real difference in attitude in these two households, whatever the motive, and it is a distinction that runs throughout the life of Odysseus as though it were a leitmotif.

The boy Odysseus, like all Achaean boys, lived in the upstairs apartments of the women along with his sister Ctimene, several years his senior; she is the other important female in his childhood. Although they were the only two children of the family, brother and sister had many other children of the household about them. One with whom they were exceptionally close was a slave boy Ctimene's age. His name was Eumaeus and when the children (usually it was Ctimene) begged their parents for his company, he would sometimes be excused from his household duties and come running out to them. Odysseus looked up to the older boy, whom he was fond of, and he was joyful whenever Ctimene announced that he would be joining them.

There was something scary about Eumaeus as well. It would probably be fair to say that Odysseus, the child of the local king, living in the company of his female relatives, watched over by long-time trusted slaves of the family who had transferred their loving, parenting instincts to their masters' offspring, was a much cosseted, much indulged lad. Odysseus' innocence was shattered by hearing the life story of this slave boy who was born the son of Ctesios, ruler of an island kingdom in the Eastern Mediterranean. In Eumaeus' recollection, so typical of the refugee memory, the land was blessed in cattle, sheep, wheat fields, and vineyards; the abundance of the soil was matched by the health of the inhabitants, who died only in tranquil old age. Into his life, however, there came a Phoenician woman, daughter of a king in Sidon who had been snatched up by pirates on a raiding expedition and carried off to be sold as a slave into the household of King Ctesios. There she was made the nurse-maid of Eumaeus, who was already five or six at the time. She was a delightful companion, inventive, fun-loving, and was able, he realized later on, to overcome the bitterness she felt at her misfortune to present him with her agreeable side.

As time went by, it happened (but do these things just happen? Odysseus was to ask himself later on whenever he thought of Eumaeus) that a ship tied up in the harbor one day and disgorged a crew of Phoenician men. Eumaeus, who was out on his afternoon walk with the slave woman, watched as the sailors put down the gangplank and came ashore. He saw the nurse go forward and speak to them. As Eumaeus was able to piece the thing together later on, the sailors were more swindlers than honest merchants. They were in the practice of putting into ports where they could spread out over a city, deftly appropriating what did not belong to them. The nursemaid was attracted to one of these men, and managed to meet him secretly for sex. She told him her story as well, and when he proposed to help her escape, she screwed up his determination a notch or so by promising to steal some of the king's gold table service and bring the boy Eumaeus along so that he could be sold as a slave. Whenever he went over the events of that day, Eumaeus always said he could imagine her saying that he would fetch a very good price, how she was sure of this, his being so good-natured, bright, and so handsome, no telling what variety of services he could be made to perform as a slave.

So the poor boy, all unsuspecting, went off with his nanny one day down to the ship. Within the hour, they had put out to sea, and the woman revealed a harder, colder, angrier character. Two days out of port and she was suddenly dead with a fever, a surprise to the man who had been her protector, but from which the crew easily recovered by tossing the corpse over the side. When the ship arrived at Ithaca, Eumaeus was sold to Laertes to do kitchen work while he was a youngster—he would become a herder later on. A friendship developed among the children, tolerated by Laertes and Anticleia, who were not unmindful of the horrible tricks fate can play upon mortals. They felt sorry for young Eumaeus, although they accepted that well-known dictum "the day a man becomes a slave Zeus strips him of half his being." That is why when, six or seven years later, Anticleia suspected that Ctimene was beginning to feel something more than simple sisterly affection for the handsome boy who may even have been returning, if not encouraging, the emotion, she acted immediately. The very next morning, Eumaeus was sent away to the farthest reaches of Laertes' estate on the opposite end of the island.

Odysseus did not really understand until a few years later the underlying dynamics of his mother's swift decision. At the time, she explained that Eumaeus, who was entering his teens, was now old enough to do a man's work, and that Laertes had bought him to keep watch over the swine. To the swineherd's cottage he had gone then, and there he would live. Odysseus more than once pondered what had happened to Eumaeus as a small boy, the arbitrary, abrupt changes—prince to slave, the island homeland to Ithaca, playmate in the palace to lonely swineherd. Odysseus never sought out his former friend. Somehow Eumaeus' departure was natural, of a piece with all the other accidental and chaotic events in the slave boy's young life. Then there was the geographical distance, mirroring so well the vast separation in their social trajectories. Moderns react to this situation otherwise. Why didn't Ctimene and Odysseus organize some kind of campaign with their parents to keep their beloved playmate near them? Better still, a campaign to emancipate Eumaeus? The Bronze Age imagination did not move in this direction. Slavery was ubiquitous, an accident of fate that might befall anyone; the fear and terror of its happening was the price paid for cheap labor in a labor-intensive economy. In its way, it is no different from our own acceptance of the very high statistical chance of one's being killed in a motor accident. You win some, you lose some.

Yet an image of his childhood friend stayed with Odysseus always. Pirates lurked on the seas in his imagination; they were the menace of change, ripping the weave of innocent and unsuspecting lives, fragmenting them like jets of lightning that dart down from the sky to shatter trees. It was all so different from the calm, unvarying pattern of the days in Laertes' palace on Ithaca. Odysseus could not know what dislocation, what suffering lay in store for him, nor that deliciously ironic outcome of his years of suffering, when he—himself tossed about, travel weary, a mature adult—would once again meet Eumaeus.

When he reached his teens, Odysseus made his first trip away from Ithaca and to the mainland. His mother's father, Autolycus, had invited him to his own lands on the foothills of Mount Parnassus, which loomed over the site of the famous oracular shrine of Delphi. When Autolycus had visited his daughter at the time of Odysseus' birth, he insisted that when the baby had grown into a young man, he must come for a visit. He wanted Odysseus to meet his wife, Amphithea, the boy's grandmother, and all his uncles. What is more, he had a great many possessions that he wished to give over to the boy. So with the prospect of a boat on the return trip loaded down with gold and other precious objects, Odysseus set sail. Laertes had ordered that wine and bushels of wheat be loaded aboard which the sailing party could barter for bread and fish for the meals they would consume en route. The twenty rowers were older men, experienced sailors; Laertes would not have let his son go otherwise. One boy his own age came along as his special companion: Eurylochus. This was the younger brother of the husband of his sister, Ctimene, who now lived on the island of Same, as Cephalonia had originally been called. Eurylochus was not a playmate of the heart; he was different from Odysseus, more timid, hesitant, and irritable when they set out upon the kind of adventure boys dream up. Or at least some boys. Eurylochus preferred staying close to home. Still, he was an accommodating soul, friendly, fond of Odysseus, someone with whom Odysseus felt comfortable sleeping, locked together, arms about each other's bodies, on the narrow platform used for sleeping youngsters in Bronze Age habitations.

The Mediterranean at every point is subject to sudden storms and squalls, and narrows can produce strong currents. Young Odysseus already knew about the god Poseidon, who roused violent winds, churned up waves from the bottom, yellow with sand, bubbling with fish, that smashed ships into hidden rocks—then again took away wind just as suddenly, leaving ships stalled on the glassy sea until the sailors had to make do with oars for any progress. This was the same god who grasped the very foundations of the earth and shook them until the ground beneath roared, a noise that could be compared to no human sound, perhaps a kind of roar from a giant man whose belly has been transfixed with a spear, twisting around in his gut. Sometimes Odysseus imagined Poseidon gored, roaring in pain, grasping the pillars of the earth, writhing and shaking his supports. The landscape swayed, trees dipped as though kissing the earth, the intricately laid stones of palaces and shrines slipped in place, sometimes shooting out like a fish from a fisherman's hand. The shrill screams of women overlaid the deep menacing roar. It could be frightening setting out to sea; Poseidon was angry, unpredictable, unnoticed until it was too late.

The distance they had to sail to reach a place to beach the ships nearest his grandfather's lands was perhaps 120 miles. Because they were sailing down a gulf with land on either side, the route was easily identifiable. Only the initial segment from Ithaca to the Greek mainland was across open sea, a short voyage of about twenty-five miles; one could see the mountains being left behind as the mountains ahead came into view. After that was easy sailing. All the same, the crew put in at night in a cove, and covers were set out, under which they slept; ancient sailors did not navigate in the dark. Four days later, the ship was being tied up at the promontory of land where the modern port of Itea now stands, and Odysseus was dressed for the visit. On board ship he had worn nothing more than a piece of cloth that passed between his legs and tucked into a girdle of rolled cloth worn about his waist, a kind of belt somewhat like what a Japanese sumo wrestler wears today. Whenever the loincloth smelled strong enough to need washing, he stripped and let it drag on a rope in the waves of the boat's wake and then lay it in the sun to dry. He knew that later on the women at his grandparents' house would clean all his dirty things with a real beating on stones in a stream of running water. Now as he stepped ashore, he had put a chiton on over the loincloth. This was an almost-square, linen garment that extended to the middle of his thigh. It was sewn down the sides with openings at the seams for arms and a circle cut out for the head; there were also vertical seams in the front and back of the piece, since looms at that time couldn't weave fabrics wider than fifteen or twenty inches. Odysseus wore a linen cloak as well, attached at the shoulders with a bronze pin, a larger version of the modern safety pin, except that this had a design cut into it and was polished to a shine. In his pack of clothing, which the sailors carried onshore, was a woolen version of this cloak, for warmth, if the weather in the hilly lands near Parnassus turned cold, which he had already used for bedding on the trip. A gift for his grandparents was in the pack as well. Custom dictated that no one visited another household without an elaborate exchange of gifts; a teenage boy might be exempt from the extravagance but not from the gesture. Odysseus had with him the hide of a tawny mountain lion that he himself had killed, cleaned, and preserved, fitting it out with tassels he had sewn into the skin at intervals. This he imagined his grandparents would enjoy throwing across their bed. Everything that had to do with those mysterious people was surmise as they had never been in the same space other than the moment when Autolycus acknowledged Odysseus' birth. Distances were great, the means of travel were inefficient, open spaces were hazardous, young boys and old people stayed at home. Odysseus had no knowledge of his mother's parents beyond what Anticleia had told him about them.

Autolycus, Amphithea, and the uncles put on a big spread for their visitor, an entire day starting with a sacrifice to Hermes, the god of boundaries, messengers, thieves, and merchants, and to Athena, the goddess of intelligence, strategy, arts, and crafts. A fire was built on an outdoor hearth near the palace. An ox was to be slaughtered and dedicated to these gods, but first a few hairs were cut from the head of the living animal and thrown into the fire as a gesture of the first of everything, just as when at harvest time everything that people took from the land—the first olives, the first wheat, the first apples—was offered to the gods who made it possible. After the men had slaughtered the ox, praying as they did so to the gods for their continued goodwill and protection, they butchered it. The thigh bones were wrapped in the skin of the animal and placed on the flames, sending clouds of smoke from the burning fat up into the sky—another offering to the gods, who would luxuriate in the delicious smell. The rest of the task was turned over to the servants, who roasted pieces of meat skewered on spits, the Bronze Age version of shish kebab, after which they all fell to eating it. The smoke had made Odysseus' eyes run, now the food and the wine combined with fatigue of travel made him drowsy. He was glad that Autolycus ended the feast long before sunset.

The next day, the men were up with the dawn because Autolycus had promised his grandson a boar hunt on top of Parnassus. His grandfather told him that this very large very angry boar was hiding deep in the forest, where the sun scarcely penetrated. Like any boy his age, Odysseus had had experience hunting animals; at home he had his own hunting dogs. He had left off his chiton this morning to have complete freedom of movement, putting on instead a leather jerkin that came to his thighs, and adding a panel of leather stuck into the girdle around his waist and hanging down over his crotch. He was in a large party of experienced hunters, including his uncles. They started out up the slopes of Parnassus, eventually coming to a large hollow where the trees grew closer together, and from there into a damp forest. The dogs were barking, running this way and that, sniffing the ground, picking up the scent, echoes of their barking mingling with the snap of fallen branches underfoot and the rattle of pebbles dislodged on the trail. The trees grew so close together here that the men were forced to proceed single file.

Odysseus, eager and ambitious as ever, found himself somehow in the lead. The dogs, who sensed that they were upon the beast, were furiously leading him on. Ah, impetuous youth!—a tag line from so many ancient poems—makes real sense here. Suddenly Odysseus saw before him the angry red eyes of the boar. He held his long spear high above his head, ready to thrust with all his might, but the boar was too fast for him. He felt a sharp pain in his thigh above the knee as the tusk went in, ripping the skin with a wide cut and gouging out the flesh. The boar went flashing by but Odysseus kept his wits, turned to face the boar as it readied for another charge, and brought the spear into the creature's right shoulder. He thrust hard and, lifting himself off the ground with the effort, pushed right through the torso. With a piercing cry the huge thing dropped to the ground dead, just as his uncles and their helpers reached the bloodied youth, who had himself sunk to the ground. They staunched the wound, then bound his leg with cloth ripped into lengths—one of the uncles had volunteered his loincloth, made of the finest, softest linen. A short while later, Odysseus was able to walk, with his arms around the necks of two short fellows, one on either side; swaying a little uncertainly, he limped down the mountain path.

His grandmother put him to bed for a month until the tissue was completely healed. This posed a problem. Persons living in modern industrialized nations are so much in the habit of instant communication that it requires a stretch of imagination to consider what was going through the minds of the people closest to this incident. The boat's crew had been told by Laertes that they should plan to stay a week until Odysseus would be ready to journey home. This meant an absence from Ithaca of about two weeks, and Laertes would not expect them back before then. After Odysseus had been wounded, it seemed best to wait a week to see how his recovery was going before deciding what to do. If the crew had left immediately to tell his parents of the accident, they would not have been able to inform them of his prognosis. But then, after the week was up, it was clear that Odysseus seemed to be making a really fast recovery which meant he would be ready for travel in another ten days. What to do? If the crew sailed home at this point to tell the reason for their delay, they would just have to turn right around to pick up their fully recovered passenger. The practical solution, everyone decided, was for the crew to wait another ten days.

Back in Ithaca, Laertes noticed that the crew was late in returning. Because there had been no major storms at sea, he figured that they had not met with any mishap on the water. Probably the hospitality at the grandparents' house was being extended. The really important fact to consider, however, is that there was no way Laertes could know. A lifetime of accepting this truth had instilled in him and everyone else in his culture a capacity for not anticipating, for living in the space and moment. Historians of antiquity like to talk about ancient Greek fatalism. It was not that the ancient denied himself the exercise of choice, canceled out will, went with the flow; it was more the case that circumstances were far less well-known and implications could not be so well explored. What you see is what you get. Laertes and Anticleia went about their daily routine; they waited, they exercised patience. Nothing in their life experience had taught them another way.

Meanwhile, Amphithea looked at the wound and was pleased to see that the glowing redness was gone, the skin was turning brown again. Nevertheless, being a grandmother, she decided that a few more days of enforced rest would be a good thing. Since she saw so little of Laertes and Anticleia, they were not now in the forefront of her concerns. And a little more time went by. When Odysseus was able to hobble around a bit, his grandfather walked with him as he tested his legs. One day their excursion was to a nearby hill to visit the family tombs; that it was an anniversary of the death of one of Odysseus' maternal ancestors was all that he could later remember. The graves were chambers cut into the soft rock of the hill, and before them were clay figurines, variations of a standing woman with both hands on her head, a gesture that Odysseus recognized as a woman's ritual mourning. Someone had set flaring bowls of food out; Odysseus and his grandfather brought ribbons and a garland of flowers. The doors to the chambers were shut tight to prevent the smell of desiccating flesh from escaping.

It was a holiday for the crew of the ship. Every two days the men trekked down to the shore where they had pulled the ship up onto land; once more they checked its bottom for scratching and gouging, polished the wood of the ship, checked the ropes for faulty threading, hunted for weak places in the linen of the sails. Then they hiked back up to Autolycus' palace to spend evenings flirting with the female slaves of the house. But their vacation came to end finally when one day their shoulders were loaded up with containers carrying the gifts that Autolycus had promised so long ago. Odysseus was heading home.

One gift he had rejected was a boar-tusk helmet. It was leather on the inside, while outside the tusks were sewn on one next to the other, forming an almost impervious surface. Autolycus had held it up for the young man's inspection, thinking it would be a fine token of remembrance for the awesome feat Odysseus had accomplished in killing the boar, but Odysseus did not want a reminder of the fearful creature who had almost killed him. The history of the helmet was odd enough; Autolycus described to the boy how he had stolen the helmet from a nobleman in Boeotia. His grandfather was a strange man. Even in far-off Ithaca his reputation was known: the man who exceeded every other in skill as a thief and fabricating oaths, that's what people said. The latter talent might seem to make him the original lawyer, what with his capacity to play games with words, perhaps to make oaths whose language bends like copper or tin under pressure. It was notorious that Autolycus' patron deity was Hermes, who was, as everyone knew, the god of boundaries, but, what not everyone remembered, also god of thieves, the transgressors of boundaries. And he was a trickster god, to boot.

The odd thing was that later on when Odysseus was grown, the boar-tusk helmet followed him to Troy in a curious way, almost as though some god were involved in this episode. One night he went out on a dangerous reconnaissance with Diomedes, who chose him over all the other leaders as his companion. The other men decked the two men out royally in tribute to their courage. They each contributed a piece of equipment—a favorite sword, knife, leg guard, and so on. A man named Meriones gave this boar-tusk helmet to Odysseus. Meriones had got it from his father, but he knew nothing about its history. As it turned out, Meriones' commanding officer, who was a friend of his father, did. He told Meriones that a man named Amphidamas had given his father the helmet years before, as a token of friendship. Amphidamas had got it from Autolycus himself, who at the time boasted of how he had stolen it. So there it was that night on Odysseus' head, just where all along it had been destined to sit.

Odysseus always remembered a curious story about Autolycus that Ctimene had told him years later. She was only five or six at the time of her grandfather's visit, but she never forgot his words. The family was gathered in the throne room, and a slave woman, probably Eurycleia, brought in the new baby Odysseus and laid him in the old man's arms. Autolycus looked down at the infant, then glared fiercely over at his daughter and son-in-law and said, "I have come here as an object of pain . . ." Ctimene remembered that her grandfather paused and her parents were utterly silent. ". . . hated by all, men and women alike." He looked down at the baby. "Let him be called the child of hatred, misery." Then the old man shook himself, brightened up, and almost shouted out, "When he's grown up a bit, get him to come to Parnassus, and I will give him a great treasure trove of possessions that I have set aside for him."

It was something like that, as Ctimene reconstructed it, and they called the baby Odysseus. "Hated," "misery," "pain," "hating"— all those meanings were in *odyss,* the Greek root of the name.

As he grew up to manhood, Odysseus never forgot the fearful moment when he triumphed over the rampaging boar, nor the story of Eumaeus. As a kind of antidote, he took to building. After he was officially betrothed to Penelope, he started planning the nuptial chamber, even though her youth meant that a marriage ceremony was several years in the future. Never the conventional aristocratic prince who depended upon the artisans and craftsmen of his land, Odysseus showed his curious turn of mind in designing a bed for his new bride and constructing a room to enclose it. The unused court-yard that he chose to convert into a bedroom was open to the sky, its north and west walls only partially standing, rubble fill faced with large cut stones that were each at least a foot thick. Centuries before, this space had been part of the palace; massive building or renova-tions elsewhere had made the area redundant and an earthquake had brought part of the walls down. It was left deserted. Piles of building stone, rubble, bits of wood lay about on a stone floor, where cracks allowed green growth to struggle through, the largest being an olive tree, now reaching up to the highest remaining bits of wall. This he cut down but left the still living stump knobby with new shoots to form one corner of the support for his marriage bed. After that Odysseus assembled a group of laborers, the best craftsmen on the estate. They began the walls, filling in the rubble which they then faced and held in place with the dressed stones. In order to protect against the sway of earthquakes, which made walls collapse in an explosion of dust and flying stones, Odysseus and his men fitted in a frame of wood, uprights, crosspieces at the door, beams holding up the ceiling. The wood had "give," which the stone did not, and this would stop or mitigate the effect of swaying earth under the foundations. A ceiling of wood was constructed on the beams that ran across from one side to the other. Because one wall of the room was on the edge of the palace complex, Odysseus could frame windows in the wall high up near the ceiling, which let in some light.

Over the stone and wood, the men smeared stucco and plaster to make a smooth wall surface. Odysseus made a little sketch, which he gave to an itinerant wall painter for execution: monkeys frolicking amid palm fronds with birds flitting overhead. Penelope had a pet monkey, he remembered, and the painter suggested the palm fronds. There were other rooms in the palace with painted birds and he asked the painter to copy these. The monkeys would be brown and white, the birds blue, the palms green with red fruits sitting among the leaves, and the background yellow. The frame of the door was to be decorated with columns painted into the plaster, and above it painted pink griffins stood guard as though they were sitting on the wood crosspiece.

Odysseus also paced the stuccoed ground, pointing to spots where he wanted rosettes to be painted, which his artist used for points of reference to fill in small painted squares of dolphins, squid, starfish, and swaying reeds. Over in the corner of the room they fashioned a terra-cotta tub, with a hole going directly into the earth to empty out the water. It stood high above the floor on a platform of two levels of stones. Odysseus himself participated in the building process, putting as much strength into it as he could, sometimes waving away the slaves who meant to assist. Let them call him crazy like his father who was always working in his orchard; he was never so content as when fitting out the pieces of wood he had sawed or hewn for the joining pieces. He hated being interrupted for meetings. Standing at his father's side talking to advisers, his mind wandered to the wood and stone. There was something about joining the pieces together, about organizing order out of chaos or disparate bits, that gave Odysseus substance. He wanted a defense against the Eumaeus story—a life ruled by chance, arbitrary, forces of doom, loss of home, family, friends, betrayed by a caregiver. Carpentry, masonry, setting stone in secure balances—these were his defense against that chaos.

Yet any sudden glance at the scar just above his knee made him go cold. He remembered the boar's angry red eyes, heard again the guttural rumble through the snout as it charged. In that moment, in the recollection of it, Odysseus raised his arm as though to shake it off, once again feeling the malign force pulling at his arm, making it heavy. And yet, there it was—this, too, he could remember—that heavy bristly body falling to the ground with a thud. Frenzy, anger, and madness averted, the sweetness of the silence when every muscle is still braced for catastrophe, that is what he recalled, assigning to that recollection a god's benign presence, the agency of protection.

Working out in the open as Odysseus did was a different experience in the Bronze Age. The modern must somehow imagine a world before the combustion engine, before electricity, before skies were filled with a constant whine, the land enveloped in a constant roar, houses with loud voices or music emanating from boxes. Just a silence in which grasses crackled underfoot, a cricket deafened a man, leaves rubbed together in a chance breeze, and the voice of a god whispered softly. It was when he was working on the room, hands callused from the pounding and joining, that Odysseus—when he stepped back to look at what he was doing—sensed the whisper. It was Athena, he was sure of it, the craftsman's god, purveyor of strategy or plan, battle or building: her intelligence, her sense of order and structure, was the unseen energy guiding him, exercising his mind. He made a silent prayer to her and to Hephaestus, the god of the forge, who stood with her in the cult shrines devoted to artisans. As the room grew, Odysseus sensed Athena more; she stood beside him, her shield offering him support.

Another powerful female deity stood over the island of Ithaca: the goddess Demeter, whose power was in the growing things, the soil, the seed, the tree, the grass. She regulated the seasons with Persephone, her daughter, who joined her husband Hades in the Underworld every year for three months while earth went dead in lamentation. Sacrifices to Demeter often included prayers to Zeus in his role of rain god so that the agricultural season would be rich. When Odysseus was a boy, Laertes organized an orchard and vineyard for the lad, and he took the boy through the land, naming the varieties for him, pear trees, apple trees, fig trees. The king had always been a farmer at heart. Since his youth, he was personally involved in the farming of his lands; he knew every part of Ithaca, the adjoining islands, as well as his mainland domain. Rocky Ithaca's steep slopes were best suited for growing grapes, from which the king's men made a rich, dark red wine. It was always drunk young because, without the knowledge of corkage, men of antiquity could not age wines successfully. Olive trees were everywhere there was soil to grow them, from which came the fruit, but more important the oil. The first pressing of the olives yielded the oil for cooking, the second the oil rubbed on the body after bathing and then scraped off, a skin softener and exfoliant par excellence, and the third pressing yielded oil for lamplight. Steep lands were also the natural landscape for goats, from which the palace got its cheese and milk. Pigs and cows were raised on the flat land, fewer on the islands than on the mainland where large flat fields also sustained barley and wheat from which was made the all-important daily bread. The king's men were continually shipping food by boat across the water from the mainland to Ithaca. The sea itself yielded up a wide variety of fish that fishermen brought to the king's table. Near the palace itself were vegetable gardens producing greens. Salad, cheese, olive oil, bread, olives, and wine—this has remained the staple Mediterranean diet for thousands of years. It was daily fare in Odysseus' day, except for the occasional cut of meat turned on the spit and sliced off. Meat was ceremonial food to be eaten more often than not at the time of a religious sacrifice, which centered on the killing of an animal.

Odysseus was older than his peers when he married. As a boy he had begun to learn to oversee the work of the palace and the farmlands. As a teenager he was nudged toward the throne by his mother, Anticleia. It was she, in fact, who persuaded her husband to send their son when he was no more than seventeen on an expedition to Messene in the interior of the southern Peloponnesus, a distance of more than 150 miles, to negotiate with the Messenians over a debt, money owed for cattle stolen along with their herdsmen from the lands of King Laertes. He returned home successful, displaying for his parents the requisite gifts he had received from the king of Messene. He had also acquired a beautifully decorated bow with a set of brilliantly shining arrows, a gift from a young prince named Iphitus whom he had befriended at the court in Messene and to whom he himself had given a special spear and inlaid sword. It was this very bow, stored away for all the years Odysseus was gone from home, that would become the ill-fated test of strength for the suitors who thronged the palace. Now Odysseus' parents were proud of their son for the gift of the bow. Not only had he held his own in negotiations with the Messenians, but he had received the princely gift of a bow, more valuable than what he had given Iphitus. In the elaborate rules of exchange that prevailed at the time, the disparity in value in the gifts acknowledged the relative ranking of the young men in their own eyes as well as society's.

King Laertes was a gentle man, who led with a timid, worried smile, hoping for friendly cooperation for what needed doing; one would not say he was exactly kingly. When the parents sensed the toughness in Odysseus as the boy became a young man, Laertes gradually began to distance himself from managing things, from ruling. He was the king, of course—he sat on the throne when formal discussions took place, but everyone could see his heart was no longer engaged, if indeed it ever had been. More and more he openly deferred to Odysseus. At twenty-one Odysseus was king in all but name; he was now ruler, landlord, overseer. He put off marriage to learn these tasks well.

The delay in marriage was not all due to Laertes' inactivity. Odysseus had settled on a bride for whom he had to wait. Penelope was the daughter of Icarius, the brother of Tyndareus, king of Sparta, who was not only the father of Clytemnestra but the nominal although not actual father of Helen (born of her mother Leda's seduction by Zeus in the form of a swan). Penelope was worth waiting for. Odysseus had been over to the mainland to Sparta when every young man of the Mycenaean nobility thought himself eligible to become the husband of Helen. The young man from Ithaca had not been so innocent or simple-minded to imagine that Tyndareus was going to give his legendary beauty of a daughter to a nonentity from nowhere. He thought of his mother's notorious and eccentric father, Autolycus, part of the baggage he brought as a suitor. Odysseus smiled to himself at his parents' naïve pretensions for him as he watched the elegant, lordly Tyndareus move among these young men, his brother Icarius and his favorite hunting hound trotting at his heels. That evening Odysseus gazed out from the walls of Sparta at the tilled fields that reached to the mountains in the distance, and looked back at the palace behind him. It was certainly not Ithaca. He turned to look at Tyndareus, who was also on the walls—this king was certainly not Laertes. Out of place as he felt, Odysseus was glad to have come; he had been curious to see Sparta and he wanted to see how these hungry males would behave.

Now he was interested to discover that Tyndareus had a problem the king had not foreseen. The palace was filled with suitors, the powerful, aristocratic young men from the whole of the Mycenaean world, young bloods whom Tyndareus himself had invited to come together to compete for Helen's hand. In the best of times such men are aggressive, impatient, hard to control. That evening, as Tyndareus surveyed the lot, looking down on them from the walls, he worried aloud how those who lost their suit would react. Already there were signs of trouble, the rivals shoving, tripping each other up, territorial anxieties, brawls were erupting here and there. He turned to Odysseus at his side, who stepped up to murmur that he had a solution: each suitor would have to swear that he would go to the defense of the husband of Helen if he were in trouble. No one who lost could attack the man who won Helen's hand in marriage, because he was bound to defend the winner. Simple, clever. Tyndareus beamed. Odysseus had another objective, however.

For days bands of women and girls had been strolling through the palace grounds, in and around the men in groups. As they walked, their hair moved, as though waves, whorls, and eddies came along—that was the movement that the groups of women made. It was then Odysseus had seen Penelope for the first time. He had looked hard at the young girl when her name was mentioned. The man next to him had first pointed out Helen as she walked along with her young cousin, but it was Penelope at whom he had stared. Somehow he had never heard of her before, and her family genealogy interested him. When he stood with Tyndareus sketching out his plan to pacify the suitors who lost the competition, he thought about Penelope and what it could mean to him if he withdrew from the competition. Penelope's other cousin, the handsome, imperious Clytemnestra, was soon to be married to Agamemnon, king of Mycenae, "king of kings," as he was called, lord of the Mycenaean empire. Penelope, was she beautiful herself? He could not remember noticing. He asked for Penelope. Still marveling at the young Ithacan's clever scheme, Tyndareus had been only too happy to oblige.

Eight years later Odysseus was back again to claim his bride. Penelope was eighteen, Odysseus was twenty-nine. Although Tyndareus had promised his niece to Odysseus, as a kind of reward for his solution to the problem of Helen's all too numerous and overweening suitors, he hadn't exactly talked it over with her father, Icarius. So when Odysseus traveled to Sparta to take possession of his bride, Icarius had to make it into his own affair, announcing a contest of running, setting his daughter as the prize for the man who came in first. It was tedious, it was an affront, but there was not much the would-be groom could do about it, but run—which of course he did, and of course came in first, whether because he actually was that swift, or the others in the contest had been bought off one way or another.

Then Icarius would not let the couple travel alone, but proceeded to accompany them. It was obvious that he did not want Penelope to leave him, and in fact it seemed as though he could not bring himself to believe that she preferred going off with this strange fellow from Ithaca. The arrangements for her marriage to Odysseus were not that much different from the usual. Odysseus had in effect paid a bride-price, that is, his suggestion to Tyndareus; arranged marriages were standard, although in this case the deal had been struck by the uncle rather than the father, which might have seemed high-handed. Icarius followed the couple and their baggage wagons loaded with the marriage gifts right out of the town of Sparta and onto the road. At last, Penelope lifted the edge of her traveling cloak to veil the lower half of her face, and with that gesture she indicated to her father that she was now, as we would say nowadays, "in another space"—that is, in her husband's space, of another household—and she was no longer visually available to the man who was her father. Icarius had the wit to perceive that indeed she was determined to continue to Ithaca and to her new life as a wife, and he relinquished his claim.

Tussling with Icarius over his daughter had kept Odysseus from properly looking at the girl he was getting. Now they were alone together on the ship that was taking them to Ithaca and Odysseus could study his bride. She was tall, like her cousins, her body that of a woman, but her shy smile and her general timidity—it excited him so!—those of a girl. She had a long neck, her hair drawn back to emphasize it, with a face of strongly sculpted features to match it. Her nose was large and long, her eyes deep-set; he could see that she would command a household once her shyness left her. They sat together on the deck on a bed of cushions over which a rug had been laid, sitting self-consciously side by side, studiously avoiding the possibility of reclining that cushions offer. Penelope reached out to take Odysseus' hand. He looked into her eyes and thought that maybe this evening he would take her; it was really the first time they were so alone, although he knew the crew of men were probably waiting to hear her cries. The course of the negotiations that brought the couple to this moment had been so public. The sailors were cheated, however, since the gentle roll of the ship nauseated Penelope within an hour of departure. Later he decided that Athena had orchestrated the conjugal setting because, as chance would have it—the expression used by those ignorant of the unseen forces that create life's rhythms—it was not until the newlyweds were lying together for their first night in the bed Odysseus had made for his bride that he at last entered Penelope.

Odysseus had made Penelope's loss of her virginity as painless as possible and her entrance into a sexual life far more ecstatic than her mother's grim prophecies had led her to believe. However, when it came to running a large household, Anticleia was not quite the easy and sympathetic daytime teacher that her son was at night. Since her new mother-in-law was very protective of her prerogatives in the palace as the wife of King Laertes, Penelope was thankful that she had paid attention to her own mother's instruction in the precepts of household management. Anticleia had a somewhat tiresome habit of repeating herself again and again. But Penelope realized that she was very happy; she had not expected that, not from listening to her mother's tales of married life, certainly not from observing her cousins' attitudes and experiences.

She and Odysseus were only just settling into their new life when, no more than six months later, a merchant from near Sparta brought along with his linens the startling information that Helen seemed to have run off with Paris. The Trojan prince had in fact been staying at Menelaus' palace all those long weeks while Odysseus negotiated his marriage with Penelope's father. Penelope could not believe that her cousin would jeopardize her marriage or, more important, destroy her reputation. Odysseus could not imagine that a prince would behave so recklessly for love. He immediately sent a messenger to verify the rumor. A half year or more went by before the fellow returned. Sparta had been filled with rumors; no one had seen Helen, everyone suspected that she had gone off. The messenger could find no one who could tell him anything verifiable, and he had to be certain. He had pursued Menelaus to Myceneae, where the king had gone to see his brother. At Mycenae the messenger gained admittance to the palace with the credentials Odysseus had given him. He could scarcely relate what he encountered there. Everything was confusion: Agamemnon alternately enraged at his brother, who had been off on a hunting trip leaving Helen alone with the guest, and at Paris himself, deriding his manners, his looks, his ethics, threatening retaliation on all the Trojans; Clytemnestra defending her sister, refusing to believe that she left willingly; Menelaus apologizing to everyone who would listen to him. There would be war, Odysseus was sure of that. Then he remembered the oath of Tyndareus: all the men who sought Helen in marriage swore to come to the aid of the man who won her. Odysseus had dropped out of the competition, but he was not exempt. Now Tyndareus claimed that Paris had stolen his daughter and Menelaus needed an army. Odysseus would have to go to fight at Troy.

CHAPTER 2

•◆•

WARRIOR

In the second millennium, the northeastern Mediterranean seems to have been dominated by two great empires. One was centered at Troy, the ruins of which are there to see on the heights of the Dardanelles across from Gallipoli. Although the excavators and the Turkish government have done a splendid job of explicating the various levels of centuries-long habitation that have been uncovered, the visitor will not come away with a strong sense of the great fortified city of our imagination. The other center was at Mycenae, on the mainland of Greece, south of present-day Corinth and slightly northwest of Nauplion, now just a massive pile of rock outcropping with enough flat paved surfaces, as well as remains of the stone dressing, to suggest a citadel. Apart from the famous lion gate and the *tholos* tombs—and these do indeed inspire awe, reverence, and a kind of dread—little of interest meets the eye. Considering what both sites represent, a tourist may judge the remains of Troy and Mycenae meager, requiring vigorous historical imagining. It is more rewarding to go over to Tiryns, a deserted ancient site near Mycenae, where massive stone walls thirty or more feet thick and gigantic gates can humble the humans who walk the remnants of its streets, rendering them, as they gawk, properly insignificant. Here finally are the hints of the grandeur that needs to attach to civilizations so deeply implicated in the western world's first great legendary conflict, the Trojan War.

Pottery remains from both cultures can be found throughout the Mediterranean, attesting to a volume of trade and a stability that made commercial communication possible. Yet the tradition of the time talks of plunder and raiding expeditions, which in description often seem no more than robbery or extortion, more like the anarchical, dangerous protection system of urban mafiosi than the diplomatic, proto-capitalistic trading system one may imagine. Whatever the truth of the matter, war, along with the inherent instability and fear it engenders, was very likely a principal ingredient in the lives of most people. The most celebrated of them all was the Trojan War.

It began in 1194 B.C.E. and ended ten years later. At least that is where it was placed in a chronological scheme devised by a certain Eratosthenes, who was head of the library in Alexandria in the third century B.C.E. He was also an active member of an informal think tank known as the Museum established by the Ptolemies; here it was he did his research, which among other things resulted in a chronology for all the events of Greek mythology and tradition. You have to admire the kind of thick-headed courage that assigns precise dates to such inherently vague proceedings. No wonder the intellectual circles in Alexandria rated him as a *beta* (a B student). On the socioeconomic causes of the Trojan War, the kind of context we moderns look for in assessing the bellicosities that emerge, Eratosthenes was as silent as many another ancient historian. Sexual jealousy, arousal, and revenge—that was how the Trojan War is remembered. How can a war not be irresistible when its politics are sexual rather than economic or territorial?

The Apple of Discord, like the assassination of Archduke Franz Ferdinand at Sarajevo (June 28, 1914) or the Japanese bombing of Pearl Harbor (December 7, 1941), is an event that unleashed dreadful and unimaginable consequences. At the wedding of Peleus and Thetis, the goddess Eris (also known as Competition, Discord, Strife, Hostility, depending on the intensity involved) had thrown out an apple among the guests, announcing that it was for "whoever is most beautiful." After the initial squabbling, a deadlock emerged among the goddesses Hera, Athena, and Aphrodite.

Hera was the sister and wife of the god Zeus, ruler of the universe, king and father of a household of gods reigning on Mount Olympus. She had had to confront her husband's constant infidelities (who can forget Danae and the shower of gold, Leda and the swan, or the rape of Ganymede, for starters?), most of which resulted in progeny far more distinguished than either Hephaestus, whom Hera had conceived through parthenogenesis, or Ares, the god of war, a rather thuggish divinity, the only child born of her coupling with Zeus. She therefore had every reason to want—to *need*—to be considered. Athena, a goddess associated with strategy, craft, the protection of cities, what moderns would call "guy" things—a resolute (nay, aggressive) virginal deity—was quite out of character in entering the fray. Vanity run amok knows no limits, however. This left Aphrodite, goddess of reproduction, associated with desire—her son was named Eros, the Greek word for desire—and the sex act, in everyone's imagination a truly beautiful and sexually compelling physical creature (think of Botticelli's *Birth of Venus*).

Zeus decided to break the impasse by holding a contest. The

judge was to be the teenage Trojan prince Paris, who was considered by all the most beautiful boy in the world. This meant by definition the most beautiful human as Mediterraneans, almost as an article of faith, considered the teenage male to be the most beautiful of the species. The choice of judge has a certain symmetry to it, but it is not clear that perfect beauty, especially in a teenager, is all that reliable. In any case, Paris was asked to determine which of the three goddesses was the most beautiful. Given the nature and circumstances of this contest, it is not surprising to learn that Hera, Athena, and Aphrodite proceeded to bribe their judge, offering him respectively kingly power, strategic military success, and the most beautiful woman in the world. Paris, like any teenage boy, voted with his hormones: Aphrodite got the apple that Eris had thrown, and Paris got Helen.

Helen of Troy—inseparable from the baggage of a place name (even though she only spent a decade at Troy), like Saint Joan with her birthplace, Arc—was a legendary beauty, wife to Menelaus, king of Sparta. Helen was said to have run off with Paris. Males who don't take to the notion of female complicity prefer the scenario that has her abducted. Whatever happened, it seems that her husband, Menelaus, was out of town on a hunting trip. History has never been too kind to Menelaus, somewhat of a dimwit and, as is clear from a variety of events, married to a far brighter woman. With Menelaus out of town, and handsome, fun-loving Paris being entertained by Helen, the perfect houseguest and the perfect hostess, it is easy to see how one thing led to another—and off they went. As Odysseus' wife, Penelope, said later, Helen probably would never have left if she had known what a fuss the Achaeans would make over it. But Helen clearly forgot what kind of man her brother-in-law Agamemnon was—not the type to overlook or forget a slight, particularly when it came to sexual matters. For example, the way Agamemnon would carry on over a slave girl he was required to return to her father at Troy demonstrated a kind of unpleasant relentlessness in his character. But then sexual possession of a woman's body is a recurring refrain in the lives of Achaean men: a male going off with another man's wife, a brother in bed with a sister-in-law, a son getting revenge on his father by taking pleasure in the father's mistress, suitors in a long wait for a queen's hand using the idle years to keep in sexual trim by forcing themselves upon the household slaves.

Agamemnon began marshaling the forces of the Achaeans together under his command to sail to Troy to retrieve Helen and to punish the Trojans and their royal family, principally for aiding and abetting the irresponsible wastrel Paris, who stole Menelaus' wife. War always encourages that kind of rhetoric. Agamemnon set things in motion, because he was king of Mycenae, overlord of the other communities, and because he hated that his passive, timid brother seemed ready to yield his wife without a struggle. More to the point, there was the oath of Tyndareus. All the aristocratic males of the Mycenaean world were obliged to aid Menelaus in his fight to restore Helen. Agamemnon was resolute.

Odysseus himself was not at all ready to go on this expedition. He had a while to think it over. Announcing the campaign throughout the land, decimating the forests necessary to get a fleet built, and rounding up the manpower from the farms took a long time. In the interval, Odysseus had fathered a son, Telemachus, a name that means something like "Fighting from Afar." Was that name bestowed upon him not at birth but in later years, one wonders, when his father was gone to Troy? Or was his father all too grimly prescient? Did he have a sense that he would be gone long? He got the boy a puppy, the best of the litter from his best bitch among the hunting dogs out in the stables. The puppy, a kind of whippet, was called Swifty, a little joke really, for the way he stumbled around the courtyard, the way frisky little pooches will, baby Telemachus staring after it wide-eyed.

Domestic bliss is the usual cliché to define this moment in a man's life. It was not going to last long on Ithaca; Odysseus had heard that the recruiting party was already approaching the western coast of the mainland. He did not want to leave his son. When they landed on Ithaca and came by to enlist him, he pretended to be insane, not the first nor the last soldier to use that ploy to escape the draft. His scheme for demonstrating his madness was to hitch a donkey to the plow and go off into the field, guiding it in oblique lines, diagonals, triangles, circles, anything but the true parallels of the seasoned farmer. It was convincing, but not sufficiently. One of Agamemnon's men, a fellow named Palamedes, shrewdly picked up the infant Telemachus and set him down before the sharp cutting plow as it bore down under Odysseus' mad charge. Instantly, Odysseus stayed his course, revealing to all his complete mental acuity. And he was off to the wars!

No one knows why Palamedes was suddenly so clever, but Odysseus never forgot. As they say, don't get mad, get even. Years later at Troy, Odysseus forged a letter purportedly from the Trojan king, Priam, to Palamedes, promising him an amount of gold if he would betray the Achaeans. Then he hid gold in Palamedes' quarters, and saw to it that the letter got to Agamemnon. Agamemnon had Palamedes stoned to death for treason. It was in Odysseus' character that he would take revenge on Palamedes for the trickery. One might also ask whether Odysseus, as time went by, might have grown to resent Palamedes' ploy, which got him out there into battle in the first place. The fact of the matter is that Odysseus found great satisfaction from being in the army at Troy. True enough, he understood the frustrations of being a soldier; he is on record as saying to the troops on one occasion, "Any man who must stay away from his wife one month is impatient. This is the ninth year, and I can understand your impatience." And he seemed to think often of his son, sometimes starting an oath with "As surely as I can claim Telemachus as my son . . ." as a substitute for the commonplace "As god is my witness." But one cannot compare his experience with that of the common soldier who had none of the expectation nor the commitment that motivated the leadership. That motivation was a complicated mix of material gain, adulation, and the expectation of death— strange, perhaps, but it pretty much defined the military men of Odysseus' class. They were called "heroes," a word to which we have added many meanings, none of which exactly corresponds to what the Achaeans meant when they devised epic poems about them. These men were more like superstars, superhuman in their strengths, daring, sense of worth, willingness to die, and most of all in their exaggerated symbiotic relationship with an audience; the Bronze Age is sometimes called the Heroic Age because of them. The odd thing about Odysseus is how few of these over-the-top features appear in his personality and behavior. Perhaps it was because he seems to have thought more than reacted instinctively, and thus was not a prisoner of an acculturated persona such as his peers were.

He did not exactly look kingly. The males of the ruling class were idealized then, as they are in every generation and culture. Tall, handsome, grave in demeanor, lean-loined, with massive thighs, they can be seen in the statuary, especially the *kouros* statues that depict the males of late adolescence (which is what *kouros* means in Greek) in their grace, pride, and gravity. The Metropolitan Museum of Art has the only *kouros* statue in the United States, but since the notion has been appropriated by contemporary commercial photographers, one can turn to Calvin Klein underwear advertisements to see the ideal of the slight, elegant, smooth-limbed form of the adolescent male, looking vacantly, serenely, and seriously out into space.

The traditional definition of "heroic" usually supposes masculine physical beauty and power. Odysseus may have been strong, but he did not seem to be a beauty; certainly he could easily pass himself off as a beggar. One wonders what kind of body, what facial features, he had to present himself that way. In that ancient Bronze Age world, where the people were divided between peasantry and gentry, the former were marked by their ugliness. Their limbs were often crooked, because their mothers did not get the right food while pregnant. The absence of animal protein from their diet made them shorter than the gentry, who were fed on frequent rations of beef, pork, and goat. The unceasing farm or craft work of their adult years often made workers permanently bowed or with overdeveloped, lopsided muscles that destroyed the natural symmetry of the body. The symbol of this is Hephaestus, the god of the forge, who is depicted as crippled, a victim of the ur-industrial accident. It is entirely in keeping with the Bronze Age culture's idealization of perfection in the male body that those gods around Hephaestus are described as bursting into derisive or condescending laughter as they watch him limping about the palace of Zeus on Olympus. Heroic persons did not work, they exercised; their musculature represented harmony, grace, and power. Their special height and body profile were the hallmarks of aristocratic men. On the field of battle they were taller and more imposing still, wearing shining bronze helmets from which rose tall plumes of horsehair waving menacingly as they moved.

Odysseus probably looked more like Henry VIII, a chunky fellow noted for massive calves, thighs, chest, upper arms, and a relatively short stature. Odysseus stood out for the way he looked, idio-syncratic for his class, really. Helen remembered how much he had impressed the Trojan prince, Antenor, whom she heard once com-paring Odysseus with her husband, Menelaus. It was on a day when old King Priam had gathered with Helen and some Trojan notables to watch the Achaeans massing on the plains below the citadel walls. Priam asked Helen, because she had once lived among these people, to identify whom he pointed out. He peered out at the bat-tlefield and then gestured toward Agamemnon, asking her who the very tall man was, saying that he was taller by a head than any of the others. "Looks to me like he must be royal, is that not so?" she remembered his asking, and she replied that indeed this was the great king Agamemnon.

Then the old man spotted Odysseus. She thought she could tell without looking when Priam said something like "I see another man, shorter by a head than Agamemnon, but much broader in the chest, going about like a ram among sheep, keeping the army in order." But she did look and she was right. When she said that it was Odysseus, Prince Antenor spoke up, remembering a day when Menelaus and Odysseus came into Troy for a parley.

"When they were standing," he said, "Menelaus was the greater man, outstanding with his broad shoulders, but when they were seated, Odysseus seemed the more majestic."

Which is to say, Antenor tells us that Odysseus could com-mand by force of personality. Maybe it's the impression of the ancient Greek statuary, but one thinks of heroic males in a standing position, as we do contemporary sports figures, since it is the mass and height of their bodies that give them natural dominance. Only royals can sit and command, which makes Antenor's image of the seated Odysseus special. It goes with Priam's likening Odysseus to a ram.

"When Menelaus spoke," Antenor continued, "he was quick, lucid, got right to the point, even though he was a youngish man. When Odysseus got up, he would stand there, staring down at the ground, glancing up under his bushy eyebrows, holding the staff stiff in his hands, not using it to gesticulate as he spoke. It was just as though he were some dolt who knew nothing, one of those surly types. But when that great voice came up from his chest, out came the words, falling like drifting snow, and we knew that no mortal man could compete with Odysseus. Then we stopped thinking of how he looked."

In this famous war, the major figures were defined by their fighting, their manhood was defined by their fighting, their very being was defined by their fighting. On the field of battle, the casting of the long spears was the action of the major players for whom the socially less significant men were bearers, shield positioners, retrievers, the back-up staff, as it were. I suppose someone like Hemingway or Mailer thinks of it as guts, that whatever-it-is that makes a certain kind of man run up a special energy and bravery to perform highly perilous actions. The Achaean hero who defined himself by his behavior on the field of battle was already defined that way by the army assembly who awarded him the honor, glory, applause, and prizes that accrued only to the major hero figures. Thus it was, of course, that the greatest challenge that any male would ever know was fighting against his most formidable opponent—a man who himself would be defined as the warrior capable of not only killing him but succeeding in doing so. For instance, Hector's greatest battle was the one he finally lost to Achilles rather than his pettier triumphs in killing lesser men. One can see the affinities with bullfighting, the inherent erotics in this form of dying. A hero therefore flirts with, lusts after, goes out to meet death. Always. Death and the hero, that's the definition. That is why the Achaean soldiery loved Achilles so, despite his impossible narcissism, because he knew perfectly well—how could he not with his mother dinning it into his ear whenever she came on the scene?—that he was going to die on the field of battle, and yet he went to it, just as a rock star takes a last sip from his water bottle, straightens his shoulders, and marches out into those lights, the screams, the insistent beat of the drums from the band that has already begun to herald his entry.

Odysseus seems far less susceptible to the demands of heroic behavior, although one must report, curiously enough, that after the war when he was being battered by ferocious wind and high waves were pulling him, thrusting him, off his raft and into the sea, he screamed out bitterly against a fate that had denied him the glory of a death at Troy only to let him drown ignominiously—no one would see him, no one would hear him, no one would know—at sea. He was about to be like the proverbial tree falling in the empty forest. No different from any other of those Achaean hero figures, Odysseus needed an audience to feel himself whole, at least at that moment when he thought he was going to die a violent death.

It is hard to believe that he was considered a major player when he set out to join the rest of the expedition, which was scheduled to sail from the harbor at Aulis. Odysseus' contingent consisted of only twelve ships. Others were coming with forty, fifty, sixty, even eighty ships under their command, and Agamemnon had a hundred. At thirty, Odysseus was older when the war began than most of the others, except for Agamemnon at thirty-five, and King Nestor of Pylus, pushing fifty. But Odysseus must have been in great shape. After almost ten years into the war—thus putting him at nearly forty—on the occasion of his running a race in which he tied with a fellow who was just in his late twenties, Antilochus, Nestor's son, yelled out something about how Odysseus was almost of a previous generation, a certified old-timer, but how he was still "in bud." However, it is worth noticing (although none of the spectators or judges at the competition did) that the other fellow was cheated of winning when he slipped on cow dung and fell, probably due to the agency of Athena, ever eager to promote her favorite. Still, Odysseus was probably one of those men whom the aging process did not immediately affect. On the battlefield, he was always to be found fighting side by side with the younger men, the two fellows named Ajax, for instance, and Diomedes, of course, who seems to have been his great fighting companion. Diomedes would choose him when a partner was needed, saying that Odysseus was smarter and more knowledgeable than the rest, and always adding that Athena loved him so.

This love of Athena for Odysseus is interesting. Everyone remarked on it, he himself thought he recognized it. It was a love that seemed entirely asexual, different from that of the goddess Aphrodite for the mortal Adonis, for instance, which somehow doomed him to death, a common fatal connection between female divinity and mortal male in ancient Mediterranean sacred stories. It is also interesting because Athena's love does not seem to have been earned, which might occur to someone reared in the Judeo-Christian-Muslim tradition. On the other hand, Athena's love for Odysseus was never construed as an instance of "god's love for mankind." That was not at all a Bronze Age notion; there were plenty of examples of divine indifference. What is also clear is that a lifetime of goodness and piety did not necessarily translate into divine favor and protection. Hector, the nicest of the Trojan princes, tireless defender of his city and family, known for his exemplary piety, the endless performance of sacrificial rituals in honor of the gods, was essentially tricked into his death by the goddess Athena, who wanted Achilles to win in their deadly duel. What we would consider evildoing, however, did not necessarily bring punishment. Medea, for example, killed her two sons in angry response to her errant husband, Jason, and managed to leave town with supernatural help; at the end of her days, she was rewarded with eternal life in the Elysian Fields. No, for reasons of her own, Athena protected Odysseus, fostering his well-being, and that's about all one can say about the matter. The important fact is that he could go into battle with a special confidence, in fact, live his life that way. That cool conviction is a hallmark of his behavior. One can see how it would appeal to Diomedes when he chose someone to fight at his side.

Teamwork on the battlefield was essential. If, for instance, a fighter was using what one might call a tower shield (a device that was like a screen large enough to cover the entire body head to toe, behind which he could stand to launch his deadly spears), then he needed a crew to move this ponderous and unwieldy item from place to place as strategy and prudence dictated. Or if he was using the small round shield designed to protect the vital organs of his midriff, then he needed to be standing close to another fellow so that, if possible, his right flank was also protected as he raised his arm to hurl his weapon. If he was fighting from a chariot, then he needed a courageous, loyal charioteer to thread his way through the fighting mass, as he reached down with his razor-sharp sword to stab or lop off what he could. We have record that Odysseus, who seems in some ways a loner and a very private person, was a team fighter. Once, when Hector was on one of his rampages cutting through the Achaean forces like a giant scythe goes through a meadow of wheat, Odysseus called out to Diomedes to make a stand alongside him. The two fought off the challenge together until an arrow in the leg took Diomedes out—legs were covered with curved metal plates but where they joined there was always a gap—and Odysseus fought on even more vigorously, fought like a boar, they said, as some others carried Diomedes out of battle. Then Odysseus himself took a spear in the torso—the metal breastplate inevitably exposed the skin where its pieces tied together—but he realized right away that it had not hit the vital organs; thanks to Athena, he was sure of it. But he was faint, losing a lot of blood, and Ajax ran over to cover for him while Menelaus led him out of battle. A year or so later it was he, Odysseus, who warded off the Trojans, while Ajax had the sad task of carrying the body of Achilles out of battle.

Nevertheless, Odysseus was a prudent fighter. Take his attitude toward Nestor. The old man was irrepressible, always out in the fray, although it was not too clear what he accomplished, at least when his son Antilochus was not around. Odysseus had mixed feelings about Nestor. There was a time in the heat of battle when Diomedes was trying to rescue the old king, who had found himself outmaneuvered and in his confused way was in danger of being stampeded by the enemy. Odysseus went charging by in his chariot intent on another action. Diomedes signaled but Odysseus chose to ignore him by keeping his eyes fixed elsewhere. Nestor wasn't worth the risk.

You hear military men talking about having the fire in one's belly. Diomedes could be heard to say that if Agamemnon wanted to call it quits and go home, then it would suit Diomedes fine—he and Sthenelus, his charioteer and buddy, would fight on alone, if need be to the end. Achilles had the same sentimental, romantic urge, talking about himself and Patroclus, just the two of them alone, fighting on. Even old Nestor was drunk on war. Once at a rally, he was heard shouting out to the men that when they breached the walls of Troy, they would all have the Trojan wives to rape. This was to avenge, he said, poor Helen's desperate wish to leave the Trojans, avenge her tears and longing. One has to admire the old man's smooth translation of that lady's carefree mad dash for the welcoming caress of her lover's arms into the rape and imprisonment of a virtuous Achaean wife. Odysseus could certainly talk this way, but he did not think that way and did not allow himself to become drunk on his own rhetoric. Play it as it lays, that seems more Odysseus' way of thinking. Once, when Nestor had marveled at some horses that Diomedes and Odysseus had captured from the Trojans in a night raid, saying "A god must have given you those horses!," Odysseus drily replied, "A god could have given us far better horses than these if he were in a horse-giving mood." It is easy to see why his fellow officers called him brilliant or cunning. There was something cold, something calculating they sensed about him. Intelligent people will always invite suspicion.

They called him ruthless too, even sometimes, when his grandfather Autolycus came up in conversation, greedy. All these attributes came together one night when Odysseus had set out reconnoitering with Diomedes, their plan being to head across the lines into the camp of some newly arrived Trojan allies. It was a dangerous mission and no one else would volunteer for this except Diomedes, who immediately chose Odysseus as his companion. It was the night Odysseus wore the boar-tusk helmet that Meriones had given him, the helmet that Autolycus himself had once stolen from its rightful owner. As the two men made their way through the dark, they captured a young Trojan named Dolon who, as it turned out, had volunteered to spy on the Achaeans with the prospect of a huge reward. He was a green kid, trembling with fear, stuttering, on his knees looking up at the one and then the other, almost crying.

They needed to get valuable information from him. "Relax," said Odysseus, "stop panicking," and he put his hand on Dolon's shoulder giving it a gentle squeeze. "Stop thinking we're going to kill you." Which in fact they did, slitting the fellow's throat, once he had blurted out everything he knew.

Odysseus had the will to finish what had begun. Don't leave things half done, that was certainly his philosophy. "Much enduring" was another way his fellow officers spoke of him—tenacious, you might say. He was close to Agamemnon; the family connection through marriage (Penelope was cousin to Clytemnestra) probably helped. Being close meant he had to put up with Agamemnon a lot all the years of the war, including sharing the evening meal with him at his headquarters. Dinner was a plate loaded with half-cooked or overcooked meat—almost a nightly occurrence—and involved listening once again to Agamemnon's worries, to Menelaus' whining, to Nestor's interminable stories of his prowess in battle thirty or more years earlier, and lord knows what else. However, the occasion was so loaded with symbolic value that missing a night by choice was as reckless as not being invited was horrifying. Odysseus behaved toward Agamemnon, his commander in chief, with, as they always say in personnel reports, unfailing cooperation. There are a couple of recorded outbursts that make it hard to believe that he thought well of the man; it was the king, not the man, who had his unfailing cooperation. He believed in hierarchy, and Agamemnon was just lucky enough to be Odysseus' king, as was dramatically revealed one day when anarchy erupted among the troops. Then, as always, Odysseus was ready to defend rank as the natural order of things.

The men were out on the plain listening to Agamemnon giving one of his speeches. It was right after the blowup with Achilles, who had gone off to his tent where he was hiding out and sulking.

He had shouted to Agamemnon as he was leaving that he would never fight again, swore it; rumors were spreading through the camp like ground fog at night. It was probably what propelled Agamemnon out of his headquarters and up onto the podium. He had all the senior officers standing next to him; this was the moment for some demonstration of authority. Then Agamemnon was witless enough, gutless enough, or maybe just plain tired and plaintive enough, or even maybe cunning enough (cunning? Odysseus who was standing next to Agamemnon could not read it in his face) to tell the assembled army they might as well go home. If he had been planning to test them, he badly misjudged. It was the tenth year they had been fighting out in front of the walls of Troy, and they were no closer to success than the day they arrived. Agamemnon's words were scarcely out of his mouth when there was a roar that echoed back from the hills and the men were off as though it were a race, pushing and shoving to get ahead of one another, running for the ships pulled up on the beach. No matter that some of the hulls were warped, losing planks, oars were lost, rot was setting in. The more desperate were even starting to climb up, slipping, losing their toehold as they swung on the ropes hanging over the sides.

At that moment, as he claimed later, a voice rang out in Odysseus' head: "Stop them." He knew immediately it was Athena. Quick as an arrow, Odysseus snatched the royal scepter from Agamemnon's hand, and sped through the jumble of shouting, sweating men striking with his staff whomever he perceived was an ordinary soldier.

"Get back, you cowards"—he hurled the staff about, striking right and left—"sit down and listen to your betters. We can't all be kings here and make decisions. There must be one king, one man to whom the god Zeus has given the scepter and the power of decision."

Of course, if it was one of the nobility springing along on his muscled, long legs, Odysseus would speak in quite another way: "Stop, sir, don't run and set a bad example. You have no idea what Agamemnon has in mind. It may go very bad for you, this flight pell-mell to the beach. Better to turn back and get the soldiers to follow you."

Odysseus went about marshaling the volatile army himself, resorting to violence when he had to. For instance, a man named Thersites, a common soldier of the ranks and, like so many of the underclass, physically malformed, with a brute and ugly face, was obviously sharp, intelligent, highly verbal, and perceptive enough to be angry at the accepted social order. When the army was more or less calmed, the flock of sheep nudged into position by Odysseus the sheepdog, and quieting down so the speeches could continue, Thersites would not stop abusing Agamemnon, shouting out at the top of his lungs, how unjust it was that the great king took so large a share of the plunder when his efforts at getting it did not match the struggle of the common soldiery. Like lightning Odysseus split the crowd asunder, rushing to Thersites' side, where he gave him a humiliating tongue lashing, then raised the golden scepter and finished with blows to the poor man's head and shoulders hard enough to draw blood. There was silence, then a moan and muffled crying from Thersites and embarrassed snickers from his fellow soldiers. Once order again had been restored Odysseus made his way to the front. He stood looking out at the army still holding Agamemnon's scepter of state; standing next to him, he realized, was Athena in disguise as the herald Talthybius. If the real king could not perform his role, then Odysseus would stand in for him. He even harangued the troops with a speech that was upbeat and encouraging, the very opposite of what Agamemnon had said at the start of the assembly.

One king, one lord appointed by Zeus. Well, it was not Odysseus' fault that the king of the citadel of Mycenae, overlord of them all, was Agamemnon. Truth to tell, after that, when Agamemnon died, the system pretty much died with him; the constant anarchy among the leaders at Troy was a hint that change was under way. That the Mycenaean empire must already have been disintegrating seems clear from the story told by Odysseus and Ctimene's childhood comrade, the slave boy Eumaeus: when you have pirates operating openly on the seas, it is evident that stable lines of communication have broken down. By the time Odysseus made it home, which was twenty years after he had left, anything like an empire was only a memory. No grand ruler anymore; just a collection of country squires calling themselves "kings," each in his own little fertile valley ringed by mountains or on his own little "sea-girt" island.

But at Troy, with a war going on, Odysseus was promoting hierarchy and however weak or vain or arrogant, Agamemnon was at the apex. Sometimes the leader's behavior still rocked Odysseus' customary composure. Once, when the men were poised to go out into battle formation, the trumpets had sounded, and units were moving forward, Agamemnon decided to review the divisions. He arrived where some at the back had yet to hear the call. There was Odysseus standing at rest, his troops idling, talking to one another, leaning on their weapons. Agamemnon shouted out nastily that Odysseus was always right there first at the buffet table at the officers' mess, now why in the hell wasn't he out there in front rallying his troops? Agamemnon couldn't stop himself, but had to go on about Odysseus being a cheat, how greedy he was, until suddenly Odysseus, enraged, like a farm dog eyeing a stranger on the road, turned on him. Those around him knew he was seriously angry when his assertions were prefaced "as the father of Telemachus"; it was always a test of his intensity. Agamemnon tried to gain the upper hand by laughing, at the same time discounting the nasty remarks he had made, and then stating that he knew deep down inside Odysseus had only mellow thoughts. It was a strange performance, that. Then, like the weakling he was, Agememnon turned on Diomedes, who was also way at the back and standing quietly, just waiting his turn. Diomedes was a much younger man, and he never was one to rock the boat, so he shrugged and apologized to Agamemnon. That soothed the so-called lord of men, and things returned to normal. It was about the only time that Odysseus let his true feelings show in front of his soldiers. His public stance was one king, one lord, sceptered from Zeus.

But on another occasion, when none of the common soldiery was witness, he dropped any pretension of respect for the leader. The issue this time, clear enough, was not his contempt for Agamemnon so much as his concern that the Achaean leader was ready to give up the fight. It was a parley of the high command and Agamemnon was having the vapors, so to speak; he as much as said they should flee to the ships already in the water, then, under the cover of darkness that night, come back to get the beached ships into the water. If they could, he said; he was ready to leave the common soldiery to die while running interference, that's what it amounted to. Suddenly Odysseus lashed out at him, the others remembered, saying what no one else had the nerve to say. No one could recall exactly, they were all so shocked, but it was something like: "What the hell are you saying! You'll ruin us all! You should be commanding a bunch of imbeciles and incompetents, anyone but us. But it's us, damn it, Zeus set you up to command, from our youth—and the way things are going—till we die of old age. You want to give up? Don't let anyone hear you say that, words that would never come out of the mouth of a man who knew how to speak sense, who was a genuine king, a sceptered king that the Achaeans deserve. You are despicable for saying what you said."

The rest were astounded when Agamemnon could respond only by saying, "You hurt my feelings. I really didn't mean what you think." Either Odysseus had exceptional moral force with Agamemnon, or the king of kings was truly losing it. The truth of the matter was that Agamemnon invested a lot of authority in Odysseus. With no form of electronic communication, not even writing techniques, the word of some exceptionally trusted and well-placed person was crucial to any mission. Odysseus would be much in demand, therefore. In the days when Agamemnon was preparing the expedition, Odysseus was the one he sent to Phthia to the home of Achilles' father, Peleus, to demand that the son join the army at Troy. Later on, when Achilles had died at Troy, Agamemnon sent him to Scyros to fetch Neoptolemus, Achilles' sixteen-year-old son, who, it was prophesied, was essential to winning the war. When Agamemnon sent Odysseus along with Menelaus to parleys within the walls of Troy, it is not hard to see that the king balanced royal authority (brother to the king) with diplomatic smarts. It was well-known that Agamemnon feared for Menelaus much of the time, so obviously an intellectual lightweight, not to mention timid. Odysseus routinely represented the Achaeans in battlefield negotiations, such as setting up with the Trojan prince, Hector, the parameters for the duel between Menelaus and Paris.

Some of these missions were deeply compromising. When the winds died down at Aulis, and Calchas, the priest of Apollo, declared to Agamemnon that the gods demanded the sacrifice of his daughter Iphigenia to appease them and restore the wind to fill the sails, the king pretended that he had arranged a wedding between

Achilles and Iphigenia and sent Odysseus along with the herald Talthybius to bring her and Clytemnestra from Mycenae to Aulis for the ceremony. This last assignment is odious, or so it seems to moderns who have no way to judge the exigencies of omens, priestly interpretations, imperatives of military command, and the relative value of fathers, daughters, careers, and sacrifice as they were viewed in the late Mycenaean Bronze Age. So much is unknown, although not the simple quick eternally satisfying judgment of Clytemnestra, the aggrieved mother, who ten years later murdered her husband. Apart from the royal brothers, only Calchas and Odysseus knew of the plan before Odysseus returned with the faux bridal party. At one moment when the anguished Agamemnon, faltering, determined to countermand the plan, his brother Menelaus replied that it would be easy enough to dispatch Calchas into eternal silence. But how, they both asked, were they to reckon with Odysseus? Menelaus dismissed him as one whose stature was insignificant enough that what he might say would have no weight. Agamemnon violently disagreed, thinking paranoically of his cunning and how he would work his rhetorical magic on the common soldiery who had a lot at stake in the sailing. It seemed that in some small but essential way Odysseus alone was the final cause of that debacle. Afterward Odysseus never said a word about the event or his part in it, although it is not hard to see that it bonded him and Agamemnon together in some unholy union, the depths of which no outsider could plumb.

Odysseus was asked to use his diplomatic skill when Agamemnon and Achilles had their famous blowup over the slave girls that the troops had awarded them as special prizes for valor. Plunder from raiding expeditions into the surrounding Trojan territory provided the wherewithal to finance living on enemy territory over the years, as well as being a source of special prizes and rewards for the army leaders. Men were often killed in fighting, their women and children sold as slaves. Women who were exceptionally skilled at handicraft or sexually attractive often ended up as prizes for the hero soldiers. Achilles naturally won his for valor, Agamemnon because he was the overlord; he had to look like a major player on the battlefield, everyone understood that. When one of Agamemnon's prizes turned out to be the daughter of a local priest of Apollo, and shortly thereafter an influenza of some kind decimated the troops, Calchas decreed that it must be punishment from Apollo for the theft of the girl. This really meant that the king had to return the girl, especially because her father had come to the Achaean army camp to demand her. It was bad enough that the father had been very public about his daughter, worse still that the old priest said all this in a public meeting, worst of all that Agamemnon went berserk. Achilles then grew rather sharp in his criticism, and Agamemnon replied that he would return the girl, but take Achilles' girl as compensation. One thing led to another; it is always the problem of playing to the audience.

This war had been going on for ten years, these leaders had tents full of plunder and prizes, there were slave girls galore to fill every bed. However, it seems that, just as in Hollywood a star or director is only as good as the gross on the last picture, so a hero in the Achaean army was only as good as his last acclamation and award from the troops. Not everyone took this seriously but certainly those two did, Agamemnon who could never get enough of being called "lord of men" and Achilles who was always "the best of the Achaeans." Agamemnon directed Odysseus to get out a ship and crew and take the daughter of the priest of Apollo back to her island home. Then he sent a couple of heralds to the encampment of Achilles with orders to bring Achilles' slave prize, a girl named Briseis, over to his headquarters for his personal use. Maybe if Odysseus had not left, he might have persuaded Agamemnon to give up on the idea. But it happened—the heralds did as they were told, sweating it out, expecting another display of temper and violence. Achilles merely smiled, handed the girl over, and thereafter stayed away from the battlefield.

As might be expected, the military situation for the Achaeans deteriorated markedly with Achilles out of the fight. Agamemnon, ever prone to despondence, grew desperate, and at the urging of his main counselors, decided to appease Achilles. He announced a series of gifts he would give Achilles, in addition to returning the girl and guaranteeing that he had not touched her, if the renowned warrior would rejoin the fight. Then he set Odysseus in charge of a group of five to go to Achilles' camp with the offer. There were the two heralds carrying the royal seals and symbols so that Achilles would know that the visit was official; Odysseus, who was going as Agamemnon's official spokesman; old Phoenix, a friend of Achilles' father, who had been sent along on the expedition to Troy as a kind of handler for the young prince; and Ajax, another young warrior, to whom they thought Achilles would be sympathetic.

Odysseus had had a lot of experience with Achilles. Odysseus was the one, after all, who years before had seen through Achilles' disguise when his mother, Thetis, had dressed him as a girl and sent him to live at the court of King Lycomedes on the island of Scyros. This was her idea of saving Achilles from battle when it would come time for the expedition against Troy and the Achaean leaders would be scouting out soldiers. Achilles himself described his mother's plan to Odysseus. It struck Odysseus as somewhat schizophrenic that this goddess really imagined that she could thwart destiny when she believed in destiny so strongly that she tried warding off her son's impending death in battle at Troy some fifteen years in advance—when Helen was still learning embroidery, Menelaus was practicing hunting, Paris was learning to dance, and the Trojan War had not even been thought of. Perhaps in some blind way, just like humans live out their lives, maybe Thetis thought hiding her son *was* destiny, and that was why she dressed him up and sent him to live with Lycomedes on Scyros. When Achilles had first arrived at King Lycomedes' court, the youngster stayed to himself, out of embarrassment, but it was not too long before the king's daughter, Dedameia, found him out. It was their secret, until she got pregnant. Then she had to enlist the help of her old nurse, who one night, while Achilles stood over the bed stifling with his hand the cries that sprang to Dedameia's mouth, helped her deliver a baby son.

Men notice nothing in the women's quarters, mistresses know little of their slaves, slave women can manage to contain all kinds of secrets; the nurse gave the baby to her grandniece to wet-nurse. Little Neoptolemus became just one more of the babies toddling around upstairs. Dedameia and her pretty friend blended into the bevy of beautiful girls, and the years of Achilles' adolescence passed. At nineteen, he was still a ravishing beauty, as young Mediterranean males so often are. He made up easily into a shy, virginal girl, eyes cast down modestly, long lashes brushing against his light brown cheeks glowing with a rose blush, still so soft, smooth, and hairless. He might have been safe upstairs in the women's quarters if Odysseus had not been part of the group scouring the mainland and islands looking for him. The army leaders had heard tell that this young son of Peleus was destined (too bad, Thetis!) to be the greatest warrior of them all at Troy. One day the scouting party arrived at Lycomedes' palace. They set out a table in the downstairs courtyard and loaded it with presents for the females of the household:

bracelets, necklaces, charms, all that glitters. Soon the women came trooping downstairs, drawn by the splendor they had spied from the upstairs windows. Now Odysseus knew that somewhere in one of these remote places, there was a boy in hiding. He shrewdly reasoned that beauty or no beauty, a boy would be drawn to something else, so he always slyly set out a dagger and sword among the items. Promptly Achilles-in-disguise reached for them, and that was that.

Maybe because of his great good looks, maybe it was the effect of a hovering mother who not only doted, but as time went by turned to grieving loudly and publicly over the prospect of his untimely end, maybe it was hearing "best of the Achaeans" all the time—whatever the reason, Achilles was quite impressed with himself. But like so many of that sort, he needed a lot of reassurance. He was certainly known to be impulsive. In fact, in preparing for the embassy to Achilles on which Agamemnon was sending him, Odysseus had carefully rehearsed two themes for his speech: controlling the well-known temper and restraining the strength that went with it. Odysseus remembered that Peleus had warned his son about controlling his anger.

From the perspective of modern bourgeois life, it is easy enough to mistake the character of these army leaders. Heroes they were, bold, daring, and intelligent fighters, but not exactly eighteenth-century aristocrats, nor bachelor Manhattan investment bankers. Maybe the guy in suit and tie who leaps over the side of his Maserati convertible to mix it up in a roadside brawl on a ramp of the Santa Ana Freeway at rush hour is a more apt modern equivalent. In a world without police, codified social rules, or even clusters of socialized citizens, the males of the Achaean warrior class were bred to protect the people among whom they were reared as well as to defend themselves.

It is easy to visualize their overdeveloped physiques. No doubt they had psyches, tough behaviors, to match. One remembers the history of Achilles' great friend Patroclus, who came as a refugee to King Peleus' court after killing a cousin one day in a tempest of anger while playing chess, an event that everyone seemed to take as a regrettable but not particularly remarkable exercise of emotion in the highborn young. Present-day rogue professional athletes, handsome, commanding presences, their beautiful, powerful bodies in luxurious, well-draped suits, clothes that both tantalize and dominate, are the more likely equivalents. Like a high-priced sports car that can go from zero to a hundred miles an hour in a sickening squeal of rubber, these men are volatile; the least little thing gets to them, fists flail, knives are brandished, guns go off.

Naturally, Achilles offered the emissaries food when they arrived and, even though they had just finished eating in Agamemnon's tent, Odysseus and his party proceeded to dig in. Since the beginning of time, Mediterranean people have been demanding that their guests eat, and the guests have masochistically yielded. When they had taken what seemed proper, Ajax nodded to Phoenix—the old man, the friend of Achilles' family. Odysseus, who perceived this subtle stage direction, would have none of it. He was Agamemnon's representative; Ajax after all was there only as a buddy, and Phoenix was probably not going to do more than cry a little and try emotional blackmail. Most important, Odysseus wanted to control the tone right from the start. So he quickly raised his goblet and started the round of speeches. He seemed confident. The Trojan prince Antenor was so right when he described Odysseus as an intoxicating speaker.

At the very beginning, he let Agamemnon's proposal ride on a sharp psychological thrust guaranteed to go deep into Achilles' heart. It was the thought of Hector, Troy's greatest champion, and Achilles' rival for battlefield stardom, roaming the battlefield, free of the competition.

"Hector is out there in all his glory," Odysseus said. "His strength makes him huge in his pride, raging, free of opposition, yielding to no one." Because he was a clever speaker, he knew enough to pull back from the all-important subtext once he had displayed it. He immediately changed tack, admonishing Achilles piously enough to pity his fellow warriors. After delivering Agamemnon's message, carefully listing each gift, each promise, just as his chief had defined them, he returned to the theme of compassion, but adroitly managed to turn the focus to Hector once again.

"Have a heart, think of your fellow soldiers. . . . Fight for them, and they may confer even greater distinction upon you. . . . You might even kill Hector this time, since in his battle fury he is charging right up and into our lines, since he thinks *that no one out there fighting right now can equal him*." It was an elegant speech: begin with Hector, move to compassion for the troops, then Agamemnon's bribe, the core of the talk, compassion again with an aside on glory which after all comes from the troops, and back to Hector. Hector and glory. Odysseus must have thought of himself as the hunter teasing the mountain lion into the snare. It seemed somehow that Achilles saw it that way, too.

He got right to the point. "I will make my answer out straight, Odysseus, as to what I think, which is in fact the way things will go, so you all don't have to come by to sit with me and speak gently into my ear. Because what I hate more than anything is the man who says one thing with his mouth while he thinks something else in his heart." Achilles was having none of it. Straight out, the way things will go, that was what he wanted in speech. One thing in the mouth, another in the heart, was a distinction Achilles could not make. Was Odysseus thinking at that very moment about his self-conscious use of language, his capacity for analysis, defining and refining what is naïvely called reality as he heard Achilles' words? Was Achilles in fact calling him a liar? Was Achilles remembering how Agamemnon and Odysseus had used him as unsuspecting bait to get Clytemnestra to bring her daughter, Iphigenia, to Aulis in anticipation of marriage, when instead she was to be sacrificed? Achilles was not known for his subtlety; these warriors were not as a rule subtle men.

Achilles' contempt was palpable; maybe it had been a mistake sending Odysseus as the spokesman for Agamemnon. Achilles certainly despised Agamemnon, and he seemed to feel the same way about Odysseus. But Odysseus did not respond because he was on a mission that did not call for validating himself. It was Achilles' need for validation that he was addressing: recompense and glory. He had put it as well as he could. Indeed, the meeting ended in failure; Achilles would not yield, not for Agamemnon's gifts, not for Phoenix's tears, not for Ajax's buddy talk. Odysseus went back to report, and on the next night he had the far more positive and successful experience of going on a spying expedition in the darkness with Diomedes, who was the very opposite of Achilles—cooperative, deferential to the older Odysseus—but just as tough and courageous.

Before the war was over, Odysseus had occasion to deal with another prima donna of the expedition. This was Philoctetes, whose story is a sad one, even though it might be said to have a happy ending. He set out for Troy with the expectation of glory that animated all these highborn adventurers, in his case with some stronger assurance: the great god Heracles had left him a bow that guaranteed its owner a triumph. Philoctetes anticipated making the decisive strike that would finally win the war. But as the expedition made its way to Troy, the ships stopped at a small island, where the priest Calchas insisted on performing some sacred ritual at a local shrine. In the precinct of the shrine Philoctetes was bitten by a snake, an ugly, venomous snake. The wound would not heal; not only was it very painful, it suppurated and stank badly, and Philoctetes could not control his moaning and whimpering. The man was becoming a liability, a pollution to the shrine. So the Achaeans rowed him over to the nearby island of Lemnos, where there was a settlement of sorts and—there are no other words for it—dumped him off. They then sailed on to Troy. Ten years later, Achilles had died, and victory was no closer; it was a time of real crisis. Somehow the Achaeans learned that Helenus, one of Priam's sons and, more important, a major seer and prophet, knew the war's outcome. Odysseus contrived a clever stratagem to get him into their hands. During his interrogation, they learned that it was destined that the Achaeans would succeed in taking Troy only with the bow of Philoctetes, the bow given him by the god Heracles. Somehow the Achaeans had to get this bow, maybe Philoctetes too, it was unclear to them. Odysseus was sent out with a crew to Lemnos. The mission was delicate. Here was a major hero who had been discarded cruelly by his mates, left to fend for himself on a miserable little island; and now, just as callously, they were going after him because he—or at least his magical bow—was essential to winning the war.

Odysseus understood men like Philoctetes, how a decade's worth of obsession over his humiliation would have made a rich stew of resentment. Philoctetes would not want to see him; the hatred would be intense. But Odysseus had a smart idea. He had only recently returned to Troy with Achilles' son, Neoptolemus. There was another prophecy from Helenus that the war would be won only if the young lad—he could not have been more than sixteen—was at Troy and wearing his father's famous armor in the crucial battle. Odysseus, on whom the boy had developed a kind of teenage crush on the voyage from Scyros to Troy, decided to bring Neoptolemus along on the expedition to Lemnos. Once they docked, he would get him off the ship first with a couple of sailors so that he could go on ahead to encounter Philoctetes. Here was a young man unknown to Philoctetes. Neoptolemus could win his confidence, Odysseus suggested, by pretending that he had left Troy in disgust because they had not awarded him the armor of his father, Achilles. It should be easy; Philoctetes was sick, frail, and lonely.

Odysseus instructed Neoptolemus to feel free to blacken his own name; he understood perfectly well how Philoctetes must loathe him. He gave the lad hints on how to vilify the army leadership, and work on Philoctetes' natural anger and resentment. He must express sympathy with Philoctetes' plight, all the while monitoring his strong moments and his weak moments, so as to be able to snatch away his weapons when he was asleep or too weak to resist.

This instruction went against the young fellow's instincts. He had been raised to revere the military leaders at Troy; they were a generation older, suffused in a nimbus of glory, the heroes, autonomous actors in history's greatest drama. Neoptolemus raised objections. Odysseus explained to the lad that he was wrong about this great drama; it was in fact a group activity and required the sacrifice from time to time of the one for the many. This was one of those moments. Because Philoctetes could never understand that argument, Odysseus explained, then you had to do what you had to do. The young man began his deception well enough, reporting back to Odysseus that Philoctetes was delighted with his vehement denunciation of Odysseus and the rest of the Achaean leadership. Of course,

Neoptolemus began to win a place in the lonely old man's heart. Once he had this audience, Philoctetes could not stop talking, his violent denunciations interspersed with nostalgic tales of Neoptolemus' father, of his own moments of brilliance in battles fought long ago, of the glory, before he was cast aside like an amphora that had sprung a leak.

Neoptolemus began to side with Philoctetes. Odysseus had warned him of this but he could not help himself. Neoptolemus wanted to be a hero like his father, like Philoctetes, not an agent of the group. The crisis came when Philoctetes fell into a swoon at his feet and the lad snatched up the bow and arrows. He turned to leave, the sick feeling of guilt in his stomach rivaling the exhilaration of triumph in his chest, but just then to his horror he heard a shriek. Philoctetes had regained consciousness. Neoptolemus would have yielded his prize if Odysseus had not appeared from the nearby bushes where he had been monitoring his dubious protégé all the while. The boy was too startled by the prospect of the imminent confrontation between the two to do more than meekly surrender the weapons quickly into Odysseus' hands as he was sternly commanded to do. Leaving the poor wretch, they hastened to the other side of the island, where they could wait for the sailors to pick them up. But Neoptolemus began to brood on Philoctetes' disappointment in him and his contempt; it was unendurable. In a reversal, he overpowered Odysseus, snatched the bow, and rushed to give it over to Philoctetes. At the same time, he begged the bitter old man to surrender and go to Troy with the bow, so as to fulfill his destiny.

Naturally, Odysseus had raced back, too. Philoctetes was in a complete rage at the sight of his enemy; he recklessly aimed arrows at both Odysseus and Neoptolemus. Odysseus tried to work on his instincts for the heroic gesture, pointing out to him that his life on

Lemnos was more ridiculous than pitiful. Here was a great hero whose sole target for the arrows he shot from the legendary Heraclean bow were the island's rabbits. There was no audience who would offer applause. To no avail. Philoctetes remained adamant, and he begged Neoptolemus to take him back home. Suddenly, the god Heracles himself materialized in human form and resolved the impasse by directing Philoctetes to accept his loss, to surrender to the humiliation of going on with Odysseus and Neoptolemus to Troy, where he would finally be cured of his grotesque wound. On the boat to Troy, Neoptolemus surreptitiously studied Philoctetes, who sat on the forward deck head down, shoulders bowed. He was baffled. This was destiny, he reckoned. How then could Odysseus be contemptible? He had to acknowledge that, whatever his method, Odysseus was fulfilling a god's will. One wonders if Odysseus contemplated from time to time the delicious irony of his instructing Achilles' son in the art of lying and finding his pupil so apt at falsehood.

An army holds together with the buddy system. Agamemnon and Menelaus naturally were always together; Nestor hung out with his son Antilochus; Idomeneus was together with Meriones, whose father had been a neighbor and comrade of Idomeneus back on Crete; the two men with the same name, Ajax, always seemed to be fighting side by side. Diomedes had a sidekick in Sthenelus, who played Tonto to Diomedes' Lone Ranger, or Robin to his Batman. Their relationship might have been the sort of intense one we note between Patroclus and Achilles. It was not that this last pair of warriors were necessarily having a sexual relationship, and, if they were, it was certainly not out of frustration because there was a vast supply of comfort women. Later on, in the fifth century B.C.E., when it was socially desirable and considered morally elevating for every man of the upper classes to have a young male sexual partner, it was assumed that Achilles and Patroclus were lovers. They made a point of sleeping in adjacent beds, each with his woman, and Patroclus' was a gift from Achilles. Like males of the nineteenth century—and even nowadays in some cultures whose idea of a male night out together is not bowling but rather having sex with their favorite prostitutes in a king-sized bed—Patroclus and Achilles were participating in a strong form of erotic male bonding. It does not seem to be the case that Odysseus bonded with other males this way or really much at all in any other way. He was, indeed, a loner.

This perhaps is why he remained so objective when Ajax, the son of Telamon, lost his mind. By all accounts, Ajax was said to be taller, stronger, handsomer than all the rest except for the incomparable Achilles. He was forever being celebrated as the most significant offensive and defensive force on the Achaean side, apart from Achilles. Once Achilles was killed, it was Ajax who held center stage on the battlefield. One can imagine his thoughts therefore when Thetis announced that the arms of Achilles were to be given to the Achaean warrior judged by the army leadership to be the most outstanding. But Ajax's moment of supreme glory was, as some epic poet would say, fleeting as the shadow of a swallow flying over the land. When Agamemnon called the army into assembly, there before them all he awarded the arms to Odysseus. Agamemnon must have felt insecure with this award—you can imagine the shocked silence—because he immediately produced the information that the decision was not the leaders' alone. They had made a random selection of Trojan women and children captives and polled them as to who had been the most formidable force of destruction. Passing the buck is perhaps how it looks from this distance. What was in their decision? Hard to say. Wanting to reward intelligence? Did Odysseus have too much on Agamemnon, who leaned on them all to tilt in Odysseus' direction? Maybe they suspected that Ajax was another temperamental piece of work who would cause trouble down the road. They were in fact right about that.

Ajax said nothing. He went off to his tent. The award of the arms was eating into him, however; the humiliation was more than he could take. Men who live for glory, by glory, cannot endure the silence of indifference or rejection. Ajax was being crushed under the weight of being ignored. He went mad. Some say Athena drove him mad as a punishment for his careless battlefield boast, made from time to time in the exhilaration of the moment, that he didn't need divine help for his martial exploits. It would be an obvious assumption, this anger of Athena, setting up Ajax the reckless against Odysseus the careful, the well-known favorite of Athena. More than that, there was the ferocious anger of Ajax at his presumed active rival, the man who won Achilles' arms. Athena, so the thinking went, would want to avenge hostility directed against her darling. In fact, however, there was no need to bring in Athena. Being the runner-up in the contest of the arms was an intolerable assault; a hero's sanity could not survive such an affront. In the night, Ajax left his tent sword in hand, babbling and hallucinating, and began to slaughter the cattle penned up as army provisions. He thought it was the sleeping chieftains; he was definitely mad.

Daylight brought him emotional calm, lucidity, and the dreadful knowledge of what he had done. To the humiliation of failure was added the grotesquerie of being a laughingstock. He calmly said good-bye to his companions, went to the banks of the river, and stabbed himself to death.

Ajax never knew that Odysseus had seen him just before daybreak as he was walking away from his mad, bloody deed. Odysseus, when he discovered that Ajax was mad, kept his distance, not wanting to see his colleague deranged, to witness his degradation. And then Ajax was gone, and Odysseus heard that he was dead. When the army leadership discovered the close call that had left them alive but the cattle slaughtered, they were outraged as though indeed they had been murdered in their beds. They were determined to punish Ajax in death as a traitor to the cause, by denying him any recognition. Certainly there would be no public funeral. Amid all the angry speeches and the shouting, only Odysseus spoke with reason, prudence, common sense, and generosity. Consider the entire life of the man, he kept saying, think of what benefit he has brought to us over the ten years here at Troy. Remember how you called him the very best after Achilles. It was as though Odysseus were trying to award Ajax the arms after the fact. And he reminded them that madness may be god-sent, how fragile pride is, or glory, how applause dies away. Today it is Ajax; tomorrow it could be another. There was an uproar, yet Odysseus did eventually prevail with them, repeating the idea until they grew calm and voted to give Ajax a hero's burial. In the end, they bestowed upon him what he had most of all craved in life: glory, but this time it was eternal.

Despite Heracles' magical bow, despite Neoptolemus' being decked out in his father's shining armor, the war went on. There were the Achaeans, who could not break through the walls, and there were the Trojans, who managed to survive confined to their rocky mount. Deep within the citadel of Troy, down a stair carved into the rock narrowly enclosed by walls dripping with condensation, was a spring with water enough to sustain the population. Food supplies came in randomly, when the fighting was fierce enough out in the field for them to evade notice. The walls had to be breached, there was no other way. It was Odysseus, of course, who came up with the way to do it, a bizarre idea certainly, but his most successful.

He suggested that the architect Epeus design a massive wooden horse at least sixty feet high, set on massive wheels. It was to be hollow, spacious enough to accommodate fifty seated men inside. The next part of his stratagem was to start the rumor that the Achaeans were tired of the war. They were finally ready to quit, and the horse was to be a votive offering to the goddess Athena in expiation of the crime of stealing a statue of the goddess called the Palladium. The Achaean soldiers went to the hills for trees to build the horse. Meanwhile, the rumor began to make its way through the Trojan army and populace.

There was a history to this Palladium. The image of Athena bestowed a mysterious protection upon the Trojans in the long, drawn-out war; the Palladium made their city invincible. Somehow this information got to Agamemnon, but as so often he was unsure how he should respond to what he had learned. But once Odysseus heard of the magic powers of the Palladium, he went off to find Diomedes. They waited for the right night, then when a dense fog hid everything, the two of them set out to Troy. This time they made their way into the city, and Odysseus, by mimicking the Trojans in their speaking, managed to get directions to the temple of Athena, where the Palladium was displayed. After the war, Helen told Telemachus that she had been at the temple when Odysseus showed up, that he had lacerated his face and arms, dressed himself in filthy, stinking rags so as to pass through the streets inconspicuously—just a poor old wretch out wandering. Naturally, Helen had to take credit for recognizing him, but keeping quiet about it; this was to show her fundamental loyalty to the Achaeans, something that when she returned to Sparta no doubt seemed worthwhile advertising. We have nothing from Odysseus on Helen's story. In any case, it seemed a miracle, but somehow they took the statue off its base—it was only three feet high and hollow—and snuck back through the streets and out the hole they had found in the walls without detection. Of course, "miracle" is just an expression. Odysseus knew well—sensed is even the better word—that Athena was watching over him on that night, just as she was every night.

It took a month to build the horse. The Achaeans had scoured the mountains for trees sufficiently high to give them the long planks they needed for its vast belly and grand backside. Every axe and saw was put to use; the air was filled with the hammering. As the horse began to take shape, the Trojans high up on the walls of their city stood in silence watching, forgetting to go out to make an attack, mystified. When the month had passed, the horse stood there, a giant facing the city. The eyes painted above the flaring wooden nostrils looked wild.

Then one morning, the Trojans awoke to see from their walls that the Achaeans had decamped. In the soft early morning light, no smoke rose from fires burning in front of the tents, no gear stood about in carefully arranged groups, the pigs and cattle penned up in stalls were loose, the ships, the ones that had been kept in good sailing condition, were gone. The Achaean army had vanished. Nothing remained but the giant horse staring at Troy with its baleful eyes. If their night watch had been more wakeful, they might have seen movement, however. At about midnight, the army had put to sea on the serviceable ships, sailing out to the far side of the island of Tenedos (modern-day Bozcaada), a few kilometers to the south. At the same time, a chosen band, the most reckless and adventurous, had climbed into the belly of the wooden horse to await what Odysseus had gambled everything on. They nailed themselves in, sat quietly, tensely, and waited.

Day advanced, and the Trojans opened the massive citadel gates and streamed out onto the plain, exultant. Nothing can equal the exhilaration of freedom of movement after ten years of confinement. Men, women, and children darted about, staring at the detritus left behind, searching for clues to the personality and motives of their decade-long foes. Slowly everyone converged on the horse, staring up at its thighs, the belly, and the great rump. Some of the young men picked up abandoned spears lying on the ground and hurled them into the wooden mass. Where the shafts hit the wood they elicited a strange hollow sound which mesmerized them. No one moved, no one spoke. The silence was prolonged until someone shouted to bring the horse into the city. It would be their new magical charm, a replacement for the Palladium. Immediately, the plan was converted to action. One group raced to the great gates, took picks and crowbars, and proceeded to smash at the stone portal to enlarge the opening; another found rope and began the task of pushing and pulling the monster horse toward the city. Slowly the inertia was overcome, the great wheels began to turn, and the horse seemed to glide like a serpent up to the walls. Meanwhile, stones were being dislodged, supports were cut through, and an enlarged opening, large enough to accommodate this strange wooden steed, came into being. Onward rolled the horse; the crowd was roaring, their cries echoed up and down the stone corridors of the citadel of Troy. Inside the wooden belly, the Achaeans sitting on their uncomfortable benches looked at one another triumphantly. The wall had been breached.

That night all Troy celebrated. Torches affixed to poles that had been stuck into holes in the stones of the ramparts lit up the black sky. They guttered out sometime after midnight as an exhausted drunken sleep settled over the city, the first real carefree sleep in ten years. The men in the horse waited, breathing in the hot, close air made foul by a day's output of urine and feces in the buckets at their side. Patience was everything. Then Anticlus shouted out, fancying that he heard his wife calling to him. Odysseus, who was seated next to him on the bench, grasped his neck hard, and held a hand over his mouth until he quieted. Later, rumor had it that Odysseus choked him to death. When he got back to Sparta, Menelaus spread the story that Helen had stood outside the horse that night mimicking the voices of the wives of those inside. To this charge Helen kept silent. Perhaps her bottomless contempt for Menelaus made her shrug and let the accusation stand, or perhaps it somehow satisfied her need to insist that she had been an actor in this, the central drama of their lives.

In the quiet of predawn, the men came out of their wooden contraption on rope ladders that they let down from a massive door, the great hinges of which had been greased to eliminate squeaking. They sped to the vantage points of the citadel, razor-sharp knives at the ready, where they murdered the sleeping watchmen, all of them sunk into drunken stupefaction as Odysseus had anticipated when formulating the scheme of the votive horse. Then they signaled to their waiting colleagues, who had sailed back from Tenedos. Shortly thereafter, the last fatal fierce fighting broke out within the citadel.

Odysseus had first rushed to the house of Antenor, where he had his men suspend a leopard skin from the arch over the entrance. It had been arranged by him and Menelaus as a sign that its occupants were to be saved. Prince of Troy, counselor to Priam, Antenor had entertained Odysseus and Menelaus as houseguests whenever peace parleys kept them in the city. It was Antenor, who had lost so many sons to war, who urged that the Trojans give back Helen and all her possessions, whose calm and measured voice was drowned out by Paris and his heckling and jeering cohorts. Now Antenor was safe, protected by the leopard skin. Odysseus and Menelaus saved his sons Glaucus and Lycaon from the fighting in the streets and royal palace, forcefully rushing them back to the house where Antenor, his wife, and the slaves were already packing wagons to go off into exile. The scene was captured in the imagination of the great fifth-century B.C.E. painter Polygnotus, whose painting of it was one of the wonders of a city of wonders, Delphi, site of the ancient oracle.

However, the goodness of Odysseus was sometimes lost in ugly rumor, such as the account of the death of Hecuba, the queen of Troy, who, when she was awarded to him in the division of the slaves, was said to have chosen to kill herself rather than pass into his possession. The Trojan prince Aeneas, who also survived, blamed everything on Odysseus. As Aeneas said a year or so later to the Carthaginian queen Dido, "after ten years of honest fighting, the Trojans succumbed to trickery, to the inherent Achaean instinct for cunning," and he meant Odysseus. Aeneas led his son and father out of the collapsing, burning city, protected by the very same deity, his mother, the goddess Aphrodite, who had set the whole thing going as a favor to the beautiful young Trojan prince, Paris. She watched her son Aeneas struggling along under the burden of his old father, Anchises, hardly able to take in that what was no more than a sack of bones on Aeneas' shoulder was once a nineteen-year-old boy, another beautiful Trojan prince, who had removed her clothing piece by piece as she lay on a blanket in his tent high on the foothills of Mount Ida above Troy the night she conceived Aeneas.

Sic transit gloria mundi may be an embarrassing cliché but it was made for moments like this.

CHAPTER 3

●━◆━●

WANDERER

O DYSSEUS WAS PUSHING forty when the war ended. He had quite forgotten life away from the plain of Troy, the large flat arena formed by the Rivers Simoïs and Scamander flowing to the sea, two arms embracing a land mass between them large enough for the beaching of ships and the camp of the Achaean army. Behind the plain to the southeast loomed the citadel of Troy in the foothills of majestic Mount Ida which shimmered most of the year in a cap of shining white snow. Now he would be homeward bound. Try as he might, he could not call up much of an image of his wife's face. He would say the name as though to reassure himself of her existence, and sometimes in his sleep he heard the sound of her voice—at least, he thought it was her voice. Even the recollection of winning her away from her father, an anecdote Odysseus had told often enough, stuck with him. But he could not see her in his mind's eye. Telemachus, the small baby? Boy of ten now, and what could he be like?

Odysseus thought of Neoptolemus, Achilles' son, how curious

that his father's narcissism and sentimentality sometimes showed itself, even if peculiarly perverted, in the harsh, furious person the boy had become in the short time since he arrived at Troy. Hecuba, the Trojan queen, had told Odysseus about Neoptolemus, how on that last night of Troy's defeat, he and his companions had burst into the throne room, smashing down elaborate, giant wooden doors with solid bronze clasps. King Priam had heard them in the corridor, got himself suited up, old man that he was, then sent the slaves who dressed him away to safety. There he stood in his armor—Hecuba had not been able to stop him—his sword quivering in his shaking hand, facing this boy warrior, sixteen as Odysseus recalled, obviously drunk—somebody said they had found the royal wine stores and had been smashing bottles and drinking just before they started the rampage. With a grin on his face, the lad stabbed the old man over and over, at least that is what Hecuba had said. She begged Odysseus for the chance to castrate him. He had looked away and prayed to Athena that something better was ahead for his own son, Telemachus.

In the distribution of slaves, Hecuba had been awarded to him by the army assembly. Upon hearing this announcement, she had shuddered, then had silently sunk to the ground. Odysseus had made a mental note to hand her over to the Trojan priest Helenus, whom the Achaeans had spared, letting him lead a group of survivors resettling in Epirus. Earlier in the day, Hecuba had watched the Achaeans throw her ten-year-old grandson, Astyanax, Hector's son, from the walls, had listened to the shriek of the boy in his falling, and watched Astyanax's mother, Andromache, led off to be the sexual prize of Neoptolemus. All this Odysseus had witnessed too, for some reason seeing it, as it were, through her eyes. He watched her grasp Menelaus by the arm, squeezing the flesh with her bony fingers, strong enough to make him wince. He had just brought Helen out of the ruins of the royal apartments to set among his other pieces of plunder and the trophies of distribution awarded by the army rank and file. Hecuba implored Menelaus to try Helen for her crimes, kill her, not lead her home to his bed in the palace at Sparta. Her importuning, that loud, harsh, accusatory voice, something in it, made Menelaus stop; his insecurities always reacted—it was like boils erupting, or eczema—when an angry old woman confronted him. Right there he set up a kind of tribunal with the two women, the one accusing, the other defending. It was a ridiculous performance. Menelaus had never before, and certainly not now, thought that a beautiful woman could be responsible for anything; ciphers have no moral autonomy, they are decorative, useful, and often sexually pleasing.

But Odysseus was impressed by Helen's rhetoric. In the old days at Sparta, he had never seen past her beauty, but now realized that she was intelligent, at that moment desperate—it struck him—to impress herself upon her auditors as someone who had made a choice. Her voice, however, trailed away when she realized that Menelaus wasn't listening. She suddenly looked across to Odysseus and swiftly walked in his direction. So emphatic was her tread that Menelaus could do no more than look at her. The soldiers who were with him shifted uneasily, and no one spoke except Hecuba, who had started with a snort of derision, but all at once chuckled. Despite the tumult and confusion of the last few days Helen was turned out as though she were about to give a royal reception. Somewhere she had found a fresh white linen peplos that shone in the sun, held together at her shoulder by a inlaid pin that was sparkling. She had even retrieved some earrings and a bracelet. Her hair was freshly washed and bound back with ribbons. Before it had all quite registered on Odysseus Helen was there, standing before him, squinting in the bright sun.

"Give my greetings to Penelope when you return. Who knows if I shall ever see her again?" She spoke loudly enough for everyone standing there to hear her, the same big voice she had just been using in her defense. Before Odysseus could reply, she went on; no one who was present forgot her words. "Folks say it was destiny, or the gods planned all this, wanted to bring the city and all its people down." She gazed behind her at the smoking ruins of Troy. When she turned back to Odysseus, she smiled, and holding her hand to shade her eyes, she looked directly into his. "No, it was just Paris and me. The gods put this horrid destiny on us two so that later on, much later on, I suppose, we would be something poets could sing about."

It is worth noting that once Menelaus returned with Helen to Sparta they resumed domestic relations. Nothing was said, no stone was cast. It does not suggest extraordinary charity in Menelaus, but rather his indifference to Helen as anything other than an adornment, a prop to his ego. He probably saw her as no more than a mindless cat that gets out, goes up a tree, and can't get down. Helen had been retrieved to sit once again there in Sparta purring on a plump pillow next to her proud, contented owner. Or like those blondes in the photographs from the 1930s and '40s taken at the Mocambo or El Morocco that show a table of partygoers, fat older men, with big pinky rings, cigars, shrewd, hard eyes, satisfied, sensual devouring lips, seated next to one of those blondes, smiling, shining-eyed, twenty-year-old chorus girls, invited "to liven things up."

When the wind blew away the rancid smoke of the smoldering city, the view down onto the beach from the ramparts of Troy showed what seemed like a busy anthill. Long thin lines of Achaean soldiers and their Trojan captives carrying the spoils of war played out over the beach from the city to the ships. In the first days of peace, Odysseus and his men had moved as in a dream. Slowly, mechanically, they dismantled the campsite they had made so long ago near Odysseus's twelve ships. Everywhere down the long line of Achaean vessels on the beach between the rivers men were breaking camp. Because the Mediterranean has almost no tidal activity, ships that come in on a gently sloping beach can easily be pulled out above the waterline. Most of the Achaean fleet was intact, although some ships stood unkempt, rotting, their captains dead, their surviving crews dispersed. These were the men Odysseus looked to when he sought replacements for the men of his original crew who had died in battle.

The first few weeks they were sorting out crew, dividing plundered possessions, selling slaves to traders. Rapacious swarms of merchants had suddenly appeared from who-knew-where, just like the rats fleeing the burning and crumbling citadel, threading their way between piles of plunder individual soldiers were hawking, all very much like a gigantic yard sale, grisly, something only Goya could adequately sketch. The boats needed lots of attention as well; Odysseus had his crew examining the keels of each ship, and the ribs that rose up from the keel to the gunwales, running their hands over the side planks forming the hull to check for soft spots or serious cracks in the wood. They were busy for days replacing rotten timber, caulking boards, sewing sails, and hewing new oars. Although Odysseus was intent on making for Ithaca as fast as possible, he had limited control of this. The ship of that time was what would be called square-rigged; that is, the sail was attached to a yardarm suspended from the mast and extended across the width of the ship. So, unlike modern sailing vessels with sails hung fore and aft, Odysseus' ship could not sail so close to the wind, making it much more vulnerable to shifting wind and high velocities.

Benches for the rowers ran across from beam to beam, supported by posts that were fitted into the keel. The men sat two abreast, making for perhaps a nine- or ten-foot-wide boat, and maybe one hundred feet or more long. Beneath the bench was a vacant space above the keel where cargo could be stored. The wood for the new oars came from younger trees, absolutely straight in their growth; at the spreading root end, the wood was carved into a blade that was much broader than modern-day oars. These oars were attached to the gunwales by leather thongs. On a deck in the back stood a steersman who used an extra large oar instead of the present-day rudder. There was probably another slight deck in the front giving a platform to stand on, and a place for the captain to go beneath to escape bad weather. With fifty rowers to a ship, plus one or two in command, Odysseus' contingent of twelve carried somewhat over six hundred men. Without steam or a combustion engine, the ships were dependent upon the human strength of oarsmen and the velocity and direction of wind filling the sails, and always without warning they could be drawn into violent sea currents or tipped to the side in a sudden squall. In fact, Odysseus and his men were scarcely clear of the Trojan coast when sudden strong winds hit them all like a slap to the face, sending them west onto the coast of Thrace. Driven ashore, they could see settlements; the people were called Kikones, as they were told by the villagers in Ismaros, the first town they came to. The Kikones, they learned, were a tribe who had been allies of the Trojans throughout the long war, supplying them with food, if not a certain number of militia.

Odysseus and his crew took advantage of this political fact by sacking the village, plundering it of anything worth taking aboard, killing the men, and bringing the women and children along to sell as potential slaves. On the surface of things, this action seems odd; one would think that the ships were already loaded with Trojan plunder. Perhaps, however, it demonstrates that the ten-year siege of Troy had left a city depleted of almost anything a soldier would call decent plunder, a dearth of young children (for slave sales) who most likely would be the first to let die of starvation when supplies ran low; those women who were carried away from Troy were emaciated and sick, maybe even fewer than expected because of last-minute suicides. No doubt the people and furnishings of Ismaros looked very good in comparison with what they had got out of Troy. Odysseus sensibly instituted a grand distribution among the men so that they would continue on their voyage, all of them contented. He himself was no doubt satisfied with the quantity of glittering gifts pressed upon him by the priest of Apollo at Ismaros, whose life he had spared, a second millennium version of protection money.

Thereafter Odysseus seems to have lost control of his men, who went on a nightlong orgy of eating and drinking alongside their beached ships until suddenly a band of neighboring Kikones burst upon their revels. Responding to a desperate message sent out from someone who escaped the debacle at Ismaros (the priest of Apollo, most likely), the Kikones arrived as angry and vengeful as they were strong and fresh. The battle-weary and somewhat drunken men with Odysseus were no match, and barely managed to escape onto their ships after a day of heavy fighting, leaving behind some seventy-two men dead. One wonders how Odysseus reacted to this disaster; a man whose career at Troy was remarkable for his frequent assumption of

authority as he marshaled troops, or rallied the dispirited Agamemnon, or disciplined recalcitrants now suddenly confronting real and
dangerous anarchy among his crew.

The twelve ships got away, but the mood of the men did not
lighten as they thought of the disaster which they had brought upon
themselves, of their fellows left dead at the hands of the Kikones.
Their depression was almost immediately compounded by terror as
another giant Mediterranean storm blew up out of nowhere, making
the waters boil with violent currents. The wind grew so strong that
they had to stow the masts and sails; there was nothing to do but lie
in the bottoms of the boats, surrendering utterly to the meteorologi-
cal violence playing itself out through two nights, the intervening
day scarcely brighter, revealing nothing of their surroundings. When
finally the skies cleared, they found themselves off the coast of the
Peloponnesus. A steady breeze replaced the storm winds, the crews
raised their sails, and the ships began to make their way to the turn
at Cape Malea on the southeastern tip of the Peloponnesus. Ancient
crews would know that here they were attempting a dangerous passage because the winds can cut in from several directions and there
are no harbors.

Odysseus' twelve ships seem to have made the turn; shepherds
in the fields above remembered waving at a flotilla of a dozen boats.
What exactly happened next is not at all clear, except that the fleet
seems to have gone far off its course—in more ways than one, you
might say. It is fair to say that this moment marks a singular turning
point in Odysseus' life. Ten years later he would be brought back to
Ithaca by a crew of men from a strange and unknown land and
deposited unconscious at night on a beach. The intervening decade
is a strange time, hard to account for, difficult to describe. Indeed,
three years after making this fatal turn at Cape Malea, Odysseus has

recounted that he found himself on an island called Ogygia, *a place impossible to locate on any map*, alone, a shipwreck, bereft of the crew with whom he had sailed from Troy. Those mysterious ten years—especially the first three—were filled with strange and wondrous adventures, of landings at islands and coasts and among peoples whose names never otherwise appear in the annals of history. The crew being lost, we have only Odysseus' account of giant people, of men transformed into swine, or of his descent into the mouth of the Underworld, his conversations with souls of the dead, events more suggestive of the realm of fairy tale than consonant with hero males of the stamp of a Trojan War fighter. This can rouse suspicions in the student of his life. It is true that, when he first recounted these experiences, no one of his original audience at the court of King Alcinous on the island of Scheria had anything but the highest praise. Still, it must be admitted that their applause was given most to the entertaining manner in which he narrated his material. People living on remote islands are furiously eager for after dinner diversions.

The first incident that happened after the devastating storm that blew Odysseus and his fleet off course as they rounded Cape Malea was their encountering people now traditionally known as the Lotus-eaters. Odysseus claimed that the ships were swept across an unknown expanse of sea into territory devoid of any known landmark; here he had sent out a small group to reconnoiter. They failed to return to the ships because, as the mates discovered, their wits had been thoroughly addled by ingesting the lotus plant, which the friendly and welcoming natives offered them. Only with the greatest difficulty did the rest of the crew manage to drag them back aboard the ships, resisting and smiling simultaneously, happily stupefied and entirely willing to spend the rest of their days in this paradisiacal place. More than one modern commentator, going by the common-place 1960s experience of getting stoned or dropping acid, has decided that Odysseus omitted to mention that he himself ate liberally of the lotus. Thus the bizarre adventures he described occurring over the next several years were perhaps some kind of mind-expanding, hallucinatory visions, drug induced. What really happened we will never know.

Others note that commencing with the third millennium B.C.E. a story from Mesopotamia began to circulate through the Mediterranean. This saga of two men, Gilgamesh and Enkidu, whose travels, fight with a giant, encounters with women, and perhaps most of all the former's descent into the Underworld and meeting with the wise seer, Utnapishtim, seemed uncannily like Odysseus' story. It is as though Odysseus, when he got up to speak before King Alcinous and Queen Arete and the rest of the Phaeaceans, saw his chance to seduce them into such goodwill that he would finally win the homecoming that had eluded him for ten years. His extraordinary intelligence, gift for invention, and improvisation gave him the means to recast his experiences into the framework of this well-known tale, thus providing his audience not only with the delicious sensation of recognition but also with a delightful variant on what they had many times heard from professional singers. Their applause, offers of magnificent gifts, and promise to send him home were the result.

Our contemporary culture directs us to another hypothesis: the possibility that Odysseus' account, extreme and "unreal" as it is, in its striking resemblance to so many dream experiences recorded in psychologists' case studies, must be a depiction of the world of his psyche unmediated by the rationalization of analysis. That he returned to Ithaca in deep sleep always impresses the proponents of this theory. Or it could be his "literary" way of describing the human condition through symbol and image such as we are accustomed to encounter in poetry. He seemed to have had the gift for it; he could after all compare the young Nausicaa to Artemis in just the way we would have heard from a poet.

Still, in the face of some of the most thrilling adventures in recorded history, these are petty diversions. To get at the life of Odysseus one must take these stories at face value, leaving behind the celebration of rationalism, which is our legacy from the Enlightenment. His account marks decisive shifts in his experience of life, which are an important key to his later behavior. We must remember the Odysseus of the war years, the sensible man who counseled Neoptolemus to accept the sacrifice of Philoctetes for the common Achaean good, the cool man who argued against an emotional response to Ajax's insane, murderous rage. Add to these images the man whose wise words on the occasion of Agamemnon's formal public apology to Achilles damped the latter's reckless disregard of the army assembly. Here was a young man who could scarcely endure the diplomatic niceties of the occasion, so enraged was he over the death of his comrade Patroclus, so determined to get on to the fight of revenge, to the killing of Hector. Odysseus counseled him to accept the gifts Agamemnon offered as amends and dine with Agamemnon as a seal of the healing of the social rupture.

Achilles, impetuous, yearning toward transcendence as always, wanted none of it. He could not countenance the army turning to the evening meal. Drawing himself up, he remarked in his supercilious way how he himself would not touch food as long as his comrade lay dead and unavenged. Odysseus finally broke in with: "Achilles, you are certainly the greatest warrior of us all, your physical strength far surpasses mine, and your command of the spear is greater, but I have lived longer, and have by far a greater store of wisdom, since I am that much older. So, just suffer through what I have to say to you. When men have been out there fighting, suddenly they are stuffed with it, when Zeus has pressed the battle on them too long. There is no way the Achaeans can grieve for a dead comrade by going hungry; too many men die every day. No, we have to harden ourselves, bury the corpse, and get on with the business of eating our food and drinking our wine, so that the strength will be in us to fight another day." Common sense, patience, rationalism, a certain distance from everyday emotion, a trust in organization, structure—these are the traits that the war at Troy revealed in the man from Ithaca. This was the man whom winds and storm sent out beyond Cape Malea into an environment for which there was no preparation.

The emotional isolation that is so remarkable in Odysseus certainly helped create the curious distance between him and his crew on his eventful homeward journey, curious because it betrayed the faith, loyalty, and love that traditionally characterize the bond between leader and led. One must perhaps reckon that some of the crew were recent recruits to his contingent with no doubt distinctly unpleasant memories—battle trauma, as we now call it. After the deaths at Ismaros, the ships were being manned without full crew, putting considerably greater pressure on the surviving oarsmen when there was no wind to fill the sails. The crew's reckless intemperance at Ismaros was only prelude to grander acts of disobedience, stupidity, and self-destruction; Odysseus, on the other hand, displays utter indifference to their misery, at least in his recounting of the events of their voyage.

Soon after leaving the Lotus-eaters, Odysseus seriously endangered his crew. In fact, he actually was the cause of several deaths, when he intemperately prolonged an inspection of the cave of the Cyclops into which he and some of his men had wandered. Odysseus described the race of the Cyclopes as creatures living apart from normal human intercourse, not even maintaining trade relations. These people had no legal systems or political institutions, and lived mainly from hand to mouth, although he noticed that their land was rich, capable of sustaining an advanced agricultural enterprise. The one Cyclops whom he encountered in the cave turned out to be named Polyphemus, a son of Poseidon, although Odysseus did not know this at the time. Odysseus described this Cyclops as a loner, a social misfit, perhaps a little unbalanced mentally. One wonders how Odysseus came so rapidly and easily to these appraisals of a people he scarcely saw. They are perhaps a defense against the experience— that is to say, Odysseus was so appalled, frightened, and repulsed by his forty-eight nightmarish hours in the cave of the Cyclops he needed some kind of rationalization for it.

The visit began innocently enough, one might say, although again in retrospect Odysseus learned from this experience to encour- age his natural paranoia. He ordered the crews of all ships but his to wait at some distance from the island of the Cyclopes. He and his men then went forward and landed on the shore near a cave where the surrounding animal pens foretold habitation. He then selected twelve men, instructing the rest to stay with the ship. In preparation for his visit to the cave, he filled a wineskin from a larger supply of sweet red wine that he had been given by the priest of Apollo at Ismaros. Odysseus related at some length how good the wine was, how powerful its effects, how important it was to dilute it with water. Odysseus had a hunch that he was about to deal with someone who would be ignorant of all social niceties or diplomatic ploys; the wine would smooth the way, he thought. They found that the cave and the land around it were a veritable dairy farm. There were pens of sheep and goats, baskets filled with great rounds of cheeses, and buckets of whey. It was a marvel, but as Odysseus was examining it all, the men of his company begged him to speed up, take some cheeses, lead some animals back to the ships, and depart in haste. They were clearly frightened, but Odysseus would have none of it. He wanted to see the man; perhaps even more, he was keen to see what kind of gifts the Cyclops would bestow upon him. To be fair, he admitted later that he was to blame for the disaster that occurred. He was slightly rueful perhaps, but hardly filled with remorse.

Although the wine that Odysseus brought along made the Cyclops completely drunk, it was not given with that in mind. Odysseus was simply responding to the imperatives of reciprocal gift-giving and the entertainment of strangers that were so prominent a feature of the culture into which he had been born. Odysseus brought the wine to the Cyclops to establish from the start that they were players in a social exchange. Newly arrived visitors were customarily always made welcome with a bath, followed by a meal. Intimate questions, even those about identities and places of origin, were deferred until the guest had been made comfortable, often until he had slept through the night. In a land without cities, security systems, restaurants, or hotels, travelers were completely at the mercy of the people who received them. The inevitable unknowns in such a situation were ignored while the common humanity of traveler and host was celebrated with the ritual bath, meal, and bed. If, as it turned out, either person discovered later that he was housing or being hosted by the murderer of friend or kin, then the two quickly separated, but not before having received or bestowing what all humans owe one another. It is not for nothing that in our time the person who hurries by, pretending not to see the homeless figure standing desolate in the shadows, dies a thousand interior deaths in the denial of that common humanity.

The Cyclops was not troubled with the social code, if indeed he knew of it. When he returned from the fields, herding his flock into the cave, he placed a large stone before the entrance, inadvertently sealing Odysseus and his men within. After doing his chores, the giant noticed the miniature creatures on the ground of his cave. He proceeded to ask them the personal questions that, by the social code of the time, were not to be asked. Odysseus replied with generalities, identifying information relevant to the Achaeans and the war at Troy; he did not reveal his own name. He ended with a string of commonplaces: that they were suppliants, that Zeus avenges any wrong done to travelers and suppliants, and a plea that the Cyclops help them, strangers in his land. The giant replied that he was indifferent to Zeus, and then turned back to questioning them, now about their ships, how they made their way to his cave. Odysseus fed him lies, about storms, shipwrecks, hiding the fact that their ships were close to hand. Just as Odysseus seemed to be making some diplomatic headway in their exchange, the giant reached down, snatched up two of the men, dashed their brains out, and made a meal of them. Those who witnessed this scene were paralyzed in shock, until not much later, after a giant belch, the Cyclops fell asleep on the floor, snoring loudly through the night. At first Odysseus thought to stab him to death, but quickly reflected that then they would themselves die over time, imprisoned in a cave with a stone too large for them to budge at its mouth.

The survivors were completely undone by what they had witnessed, still more so having to watch the grisly death of more of their number to supplement the big cup of milk that the Cyclops drank for breakfast. When the giant left the cave, driving his flock out before him, he placed a stone at the cave's entrance. In pondering their sorry situation, Odysseus noticed a stick of olive wood that the Cyclops had set out to dry, which gave him the idea of sharpening it, so that on the next night, as the Cyclops lay drunk on the floor, he and some of the others could use all their strength to jab the stick into the monster's eye. They spent the day shaving the end of the stick, sharpening it to a point, strengthening the wood by holding it over the fire. In the evening, however, when the Cyclops returned once more with his flock, Odysseus was collected enough to offer the giant wine in a kind of ironic gesture of reciprocity. This he drank in quantity, asking for more details. In a parody of a drinking party in some aristocratic Mycenaean palace, Odysseus was finally asked his name, to which he replied "Nobody," then countered by asking what was to be his gift from Cyclops.

"You will be eaten last. That is my gift to Nobody." In an instant Odysseus realized what a complete lout the Cyclops was, that he could understand and speak Odysseus' language, but he could not understand the double entendre of "Nobody." It was with the greatest relish then that once the giant lay drunkenly snoring where he had fallen, Odysseus, aided by the strength of four others, drove the sharpened olive stick, still hot from the curing fire, deep into his eye, listening to the screams of the monster as they mingled with the sounds of sizzling as the fluid of the eyeball responded to the heat. His screams went over the hills to the ears of his countrymen. When they began coming his way, calling from afar to ask him why he cried out, and who was hurting him, he replied, "Nobody is hurting me," and they returned to their dwellings.

Morning brought the blinded creature to the door of his cave. He had rolled back the stone, called to his flocks, and started them out, running his hand across the back of each. In his pain, confusion, and blindness, he thought this was the way to catch Odysseus and his men as they tried to escape him. But Odysseus had bound his men to the underside of each animal with pliant strips of willow taken from Cyclops' bed while he, with no one to tie him on, clung to the hairs of his animal, the lead ram, perched upside down belly to belly, steadfast and enduring. Once free, Odysseus and his men raced to their ship, driving the flocks before them, and set off to join their comrades. At this moment, he committed the one great self-indulgence of his entire life. He called out to the Cyclops, boasting and moralizing, telling him that finally the justice of Zeus had caught up with a creature who ill-used strangers, that it was no weak person he had there as his intended victim.

"It is not Nobody, but Odysseus, sacker of cities, son of Laertes, from the island of Ithaca who has blinded you."

His exhilaration at escaping, his triumph in his cunning made him forget the magic of a name, the horror of being known, of being a marked man. Odysseus became identifiable, someone the Cyclops could name in a prayer to his father, Poseidon, crying out for revenge for his blindness. From that moment on, heavy sea storms were foaming at the edge of Ocean, which circled the earth, ready for Odysseus. The goddess Athena may have loved Odysseus, but she was part of a family and Uncle Poseidon had the ear of her father, Zeus.

The modern student of this history might pause for a moment to consider the moral and ethical complications of this situation. Odysseus could argue that the Cyclops, who murdered his shipmates after having flouted the rules of hospitality, was outside of any system of justice and thus deserved what he got. But Odysseus himself, who advanced this argument, had made the monster drunk on wine given him by the priest of Apollo at Ismaros, a so-called gift perhaps, but more likely a bargain or payment for his protection, when Odysseus and his crew swooped down on Ismaros killing and enslaving its inhabitants—behavior that does not seem much different from that of the Cyclops. At the end of the day, perhaps, it is no more than words; Odysseus did what he did to survive. But no doubt Odysseus would say that the laws of hospitality were universal, sanctioned by Zeus, their breach punished by Zeus, different from acts of warfare which one could construe the attack on Isamaros as being, however long it was after the war had ended. It is worth noting that in a culture without the kind of divine code of behavior exemplified by the biblical Ten Commandments, almost all persons subscribed to or understood the awful consequences of ignoring the law of hospitality.

Reciprocity and redistribution were also fundamental to the social structure of Odysseus' world. They governed the evening banquets that Agamemnon offered to his commanding officers, for instance, and here as well it came into play when Odysseus drove the flocks of the Cyclops onto his ship. His purpose was, as he said, to divide them among the entire crew, which he did when they had once more beached their ship next to the others whose men had by this time almost despaired of their returning. The animals were divided up evenly among all the men, except that the crew also gave Odysseus the lead ram of the flock. This he sacrificed on the beach to Zeus, praying for a safe journey homeward for them all, but the father of the gods and men, as Zeus was known, was determined at this point, just like his daughter Athena, not to cross purposes with his brother, Poseidon. Still the men sacrificed with hope in their hearts, and spent the hours until sundown feasting and drinking on the beach.

. . .

Another instance of the crew's disloyalty occurred when they and Odysseus visited King Aeolus, who had supernatural control of all the winds that swept from every direction across the Mediterranean lands. After a month of entertaining Odysseus at his palace, Aeolus, true to the rules of reciprocity, gave his guest the guarantee of a safe journey home by bagging up and sealing all the contrary sea winds into a large sack. This he gave to Odysseus with instructions to be sure that it remain sealed until the moderate and steady westwind blew the ships into their home port. After eight days of steady sailing, Odysseus uncharacteristically decided to take a nap. He was worn out from manning the sails, a task that this obsessive, take-charge, suspicious man had characteristically refused to turn over to any other, no doubt contemptuous of the crew's skills. When his men saw that he had settled in to sleep, they decided to open the sack as they were convinced that King Aeolus had given Odysseus treasures that their leader had no intention of sharing with them. This suspicion displays the fundamental hostility of the crew, whereas the arrogant condescension of their leader was amply demonstrated in the secrecy with which he and Aeolus arranged the matter. Once opened, the sack of course released every conceivable howling Mediterranean wind, churning up the seas into pits and pinnacles of swirling water that sent them back off just as they were tantalizingly within distant view of their homeland.

Their experience among the Laestrygonians only reinforced the crew in their suspicion of Odysseus' indifference, if not contempt, for them. Again he put men at risk, and the crew remembered the risk. They landed on the beach in the land of the Laestrygonians, although, of course, at that moment they none of them knew this, and Odysseus sent out two men to reconnoiter. He ordered a herald to go along as well, which in retrospect may have seemed ironic, but at that moment was an index of his confidence in their mission. The herald was Odysseus' bid for respect, formality, civility, and hierarchy. It is only fair to say that he never imagined anything untoward befalling the scouting party. But certainly he never tried a herald again. In the never-never land in which they seem to have ended up, these diplomatic amenities were useless, indeed misplaced. At the start, it all seemed normal enough; the three men encountered a lovely young Laestrygonian girl drawing water from the spring. She readily identified herself as the king's daughter and pointed the way to his residence, for which the men naturally set out. Once inside the dwelling, however, they were met by the girl's mother, who seems to have been a giant, the size of a mountain, as one of the survivors described her to Odysseus. Her husband, the king, soon appeared, equally large; he snatched up one of Odysseus' men with his giant hand and prepared him for dinner. Under cover of this culinary diversion, the other two escaped back to the ships. No one could help noticing that Odysseus did not concern himself any more with the two terrified men who survived than he did with the one who became the king's lunch.

It was the same when next they landed at Aiaia, the island on which Circe lived. When they had beached their ships, Odysseus spied a curl of smoke rising at a distance through the trees and determined to send some men to investigate. At this point in their travels, he and the crew had only recently escaped total annihilation in two other encounters with malign creatures. Luckily, a large stag crossed Odysseus' path, which he was able to kill; he then dressed, cooked, and served it up to his men as a delicious roast. His motive became apparent only when, as they lay about in a mellow mood, full of meat and drink, he told them about the prospective reconnoitering. They cried, they moaned, they shuddered in fear, begged him not to send them out to investigate. But, as he said later, their fears, their misery had no effect upon him at all. He divided the men into two groups: Eurylochus would lead one, he the other. It was decided by lot that Eurylochus and his group would go to investigate. Cursing Odysseus' recklessness, the group set off.

The fears of the crew were justified when the scouting party met Circe. Eurylochus raced back to tell Odysseus that this witch had turned the men into swine, after serving them a meal. Eurylochus was sure there had been something in the food; his ever cautious nature had kept him from entering her palace, but he could see them inside stuffing their faces. Then he watched as she tapped them with her wand, and presto—*oink, oink, oink*, pink little bodies, bristles, curly tails. But it did not escape him—he had peered sharply at them—how they cried human tears from those dreadful porcine eyes; they must have known what was happening. He had sensed something strange, ominous, when first they arrived at her grand mansion made of polished stone. There were wild animals thronging the courtyard, wild, but also somehow broken in, fawning like house pets, wagging their tails, licking the hands of Eurylochus and his party even though the men tried to keep clear of them. Then they heard a woman singing from within; the sweet voice caressed their ears. And, of course, Polites, the know-it-all—this was Eurylochus speaking with his usual resentment of the one of the crew who showed enterprise (that is, the one who was always trying to take over from Eurylochus)—right away said something about going inside, getting a little closer to the beautiful voice, finding out who its owner was, woman or goddess. And see what happened to him! Eurylochus' self-righteous smile turned to an angry frown when

Odysseus suggested an immediate return trip so that he could meet this strange creature. Despite Odysseus' bribes, withering contempt, and finally threats, Eurylochus remained obdurate.

When it was clear that Eurylochus would not go back to Circe's house, Odysseus set out alone. He was ready for anything; he had strapped on his sword and slung his bow over his shoulder. The path led through a secluded valley, so still that Odysseus knew it was somehow a sacred place. He followed a wall of stones that led to a large pile marking a boundary. In the blink of an eye a handsome young man materialized from nowhere and took his hand. When the fellow called him by name, and revealed that he knew about the magical transformation of his companions, and about Circe, the witch who had worked this magic on them, Odysseus sensed that he was with a god; and looking over at the boundary stones next to which his new companion was standing, he decided that this was Hermes, who was the god of boundaries among other things. The young man cautioned Odysseus that Circe was ready to work her magic upon him, then gave him a root which he called "moly," a protection against the effects of her potions. He told Odysseus that she would give him something to drink, then strike him with her wand, at which point he was to draw his sword and rush at her as though he meant to kill her. This violent act would frighten her, Hermes assured him, and she would ask Odysseus to come to bed with her, which he cautioned him not to do without her swearing an oath not to harm him. Without stopping to contemplate the oddness of this sequence of projected psychological events, Odysseus took the moly and started for Circe's house.

Everything proceeded as Hermes had warned. As she tapped him with her wand and shouted, "Go to your pigsty and be with your friends there," he rushed at her with his sword raised at her midriff.

She screamed, wanting to know who he was, where he came from. Then she calmed down a bit, and in a subdued voice began to recollect that somewhere in the endless, ever-present, never-moving chain of divine history, Hermes had told her that a fellow named Odysseus would stop by on his way home from Troy, and that he would resist the magical spell of her potions. Odysseus wondered to himself whether this was all a game, and Circe knew all along about the moly as well, but he kept silent, staring intently at her. She smiled and reached out her hand, inviting him into her bed. But Odysseus remembered Hermes' advice. So, as a kind of preliminary, he reminded her of her treachery in the moments previous to her invitation, as well as her cruel transformation of his shipmates. How, he asked, was he to allow himself to get naked in bed with her, enter her, and be midway into ecstasy, when she might then do her worst. He demanded that she swear an oath first that she would do nothing evil toward him, which she did immediately, and then they were together in bed.

In trying to understand Odysseus the man, it is relatively easy to see how the Cyclops episode taught him that diplomatic protocol doesn't always work, and gave him a new awareness of the malignity inherent in social relations, not to mention a suspicion of any situation in which he found himself. It taught him as well to place his trust not in others, but in his own high intelligence and cunning. His experience of Circe, however, was different.

Odysseus, like any young Achaean prince, had lost his virginity with the female slaves of the palace, unless perhaps the slave boy Eumaeus, somewhat older and not able to avail himself so readily of women, had taken the opportunity of initiating the boy into sex. Female slaves may feign pleasure, may indeed enjoy the attentions of a young prince, be amused, bored, or angered by his fumblings.

Whatever they feel, they will communicate to him that at the deepest level it is an unequal relationship, his will trespassing upon their submission. If he was lucky, Odysseus found a woman with experience from whom he could start learning. He certainly did not learn from Penelope, his virgin bride, handed over as part of a deal, ordered by her mother as she left home to take what she was going to get. But was she trembling with shame and curiosity on the trip to Ithaca, fearful of whatever it was that men did to their brides? Or did she know exactly what to expect? Had the slave women—who as we know from so many memoirs and novels in later historical periods delight in debauching the minds of their naïve, sickeningly protected charges—given Penelope graphic details of the wedding night scenario? Was she thinking of her aunt Leda and wondering what it was she had done with the swan that caused Helen to be born?

The scant period of marriage before Odysseus left for Troy was dedicated first of all to teaching Penelope what sex was so they too could make a baby. Then their time together was sundered; motherhood dominated her days, ruling the little kingdom his. Penelope was the perfect wife—she produced a male heir. Because Penelope had served the dynastic function, she was successful, and therefore she was valued. The romantic and relatively simple-minded notions of modern marriage will offer no index for assessing a second-millennium conjugal relationship. At least in America, today's partner must work not only to stave off quotidian boredom, but to sweep away the mounting accumulations of existential ennui. One doubts that Odysseus lamented that he had never gotten to know Penelope better, or missed her for her company. His sexual exercise at Troy with the variety of slave women who came his way was not likely to make him regret what he was missing; he may well have forgotten what it was that he had at home.

Circe was an entirely new experience. She was ageless, a beautiful woman who had been playing around with men for all eternity. An extremely beautiful *nymph* one should say, for Circe's beauty was transforming, magical; every man saw in her what he most desired. The shape of her breasts made Odysseus sigh when he first discerned them through the diaphanous robe in which she had greeted him. The long, silken hair that she let down over his face when she was riding him felt like soft winds; he held her gentle hands, pressing them against his chest, and kneaded her soft arms with his fingers until she flexed the muscle within. After so many years spent among half-naked skeletal bronzed hairy males, Odysseus ran his hands again and again over the curves, luscious curves, of her pear-shaped body, generous in the hips, full in the thighs, pulling her belly into his face. The skin of her face was a woman's, not a girl's, young and fresh though she was. There were character lines formed from delicate wrinkles at the edge of her eyes, the slight sag of her chin, the suggestion of bags beneath her eyes; they made her glance more piercing, her smile more beguiling, her look of awareness deeper. Because she was eternally the age she was, nothing suggested decay, only realization. Circe was, he dimly realized, the woman of his masturbatory fantasies and his wet dreams finally come true. Her eyes could look at him hard, then change to sweet; he could never tell how. She had experience, she was dangerous, she knew when to give in, she led from strength, but softened, and put down her wand under the right raised sword. One likes to think that Hermes, who perhaps had a good eye for male flesh, had been pimping for her for eons. Nothing in Odysseus' experience had prepared him for sexual intercourse with an equal, a person knowledgeable, interested, self-possessed, extremely ready and eager.

She knew how to take care of him, too. Odysseus had forgotten about women. After the sex came hot baths, beautiful maidens sponging him down, soft new vestments, cushions, banquets, the finest wine, and more sex whenever he wanted it. He persuaded Circe to wield her wand to transform his piggy crew back into men, then plan some dinner parties, no doubt asking the nymph to play hostess and find his men suitable companions. When Odysseus reported back to the rest of his crew waiting at the beach how he had charmed his way into friendship with Circe, who was inviting them all to her palace for banqueting and hospitality, Eurylochus set up a volley of objections, urging them all to ignore Odysseus' assurances of her goodwill and their pleasant reception. He was even whining. Odysseus later confessed that he only barely managed to avoid murdering Eurylochus, starting to pull his sword, intending to cut off Eurylochus' head "even though he was kinsman through marriage," an impetuous act that his crew, less impassioned on this occasion, held him back from doing.

As the obliging nurturing female she was, Circe inventoried the entire wardrobe of the crew with her serving women, patching holes, discarding the ragged pieces, directing the women to work at their looms making new fabrics, which they then sewed into new chitons or left as they were to serve as loincloths. Odysseus found it amusing that Circe customarily dressed in a style absolutely foreign to what he remembered from the women of his childhood; indeed, it seemed to him that she and her band of seamstresses had found their styles in the oldest of the murals to be found on palace walls. She wore an old-fashioned costume, a tight, low-cut vest from which her ample bosom spilled forward, and beneath this a flounced skirt that spread out and filled the path as she walked. Her long, curly hair was held back by a band of silver, inlaid with blue and green stones. Despite her short stature, her warm, friendly personality (always at war with the menacing witch in her) made her the commanding figure in any gathering.

Somehow a year went by and Odysseus had quite forgotten about leaving, until his crew—interestingly enough, it was the crew—came to him, tugged at the covers, so to speak, and reminded him that they had once upon a time been trying to get back to Ithaca. It makes one wonder if he hadn't invented the narrative ploy of transforming men into swine so as to have a kind of metaphor of his own sexual enthrallment. To the end, Circe was every man's dream woman: when he broke the news to her that they had made up their minds to go, she was completely cheerful about it (but then was anything a surprise to Circe?). No tears, no bitterness about the lack of commitment, no dependency.

She had some distressing information, however. She sat Odysseus down on the bed and told him that it was ordained that he journey to the entrance to the Underworld and enter it in order to speak with the prophet Tiresias. This frightening prospect left the man inconsolable for hours, thrashing around in misery. What he was about to undergo was strikingly different from the previous adventures he had had during those long years. At other times, he had been blown by winds or washed ashore; his visits, often so perilous and destructive, were the result of his finding himself in a strange terrain. Here, rather, was a situation where he was given direction, which he proceeded to follow. First obedience, then the act of will; it implies a kind of surrender of his spirit that seems alien to the Odysseus who had hitherto acted out his life. Had he perhaps reached some point in middle age? He was well into his thirties by now. Had the extended travel begun to change him? Was his relationship with Circe a kind of psychic thralldom from which he had not at all freed himself? But after she gave him directions, off he went, and on the way to the ship, walking among the crew who were whistling and singing at the prospect of finally getting home, he broke the news of their prospective journey to the Underworld. One can imagine that they acted out a distress far more extreme than his own. But there was no remedy; they set out for their infernal destination.

Circe gave them a favorable wind that propelled the ship smartly over the sea to the edge of Ocean where the sun never penetrated. Here they landed on the beach that Circe had described. Then, following her instructions for propitiating the dead, they dug a pit about a yard square, poured in some honey mixed with milk, next some sweet wine, then water; upon that mixture they sprinkled barley. Over this pit they sacrificed the animals they had brought from Circe's island, one black male and one black female sheep. As the blood spilt, the souls of the dead came forward to animate their ghostly selves by drinking it. Odysseus could feel the goose bumps form on his skin as he held them back, these fleshless voiceless wraiths, until Tiresias had appeared and he could speak with him. Tiresias was to be first; his was the only name Circe had mentioned when she imposed this voyage upon Odysseus.

But suddenly there before his eyes was a man he knew, Elpenor, a member of his crew, asking burial from Odysseus, who had not even known of his death. Dead but not buried, a corpse but not yet a spirit, there he was at the entrance to the Underworld. An accident, Elpenor replied to Odysseus' question. The night before they were to sail he had been too drunk to lie down in bed and had gone to the roof of Circe's palace to clear his head in the fresh night breezes. Too drunk to sleep, too drunk to stand, he had staggered to the edge of the parapet, fallen off, and broken his neck on the terrace below. He begged Odysseus to return to Circe's island when his mission was accomplished to give his body its proper obsequies so that he would not wander outside the entrance to the Underworld for all eternity.

While he was making a promise to Elpenor, Odysseus was also keeping watch on the swarms pressing close, raising his sword to keep them away from the blood; he was like a bouncer at a club. Even his mother, Anticleia, he chose to keep at bay until he could speak to Tiresias. Tiresias, as was his wont in all of myth, arrived late and after the fact, and when he had drunk the blood, he spoke with that characteristic ambiguity that kept his prestige so great among Greek-speaking persons for centuries. He warned Odysseus that there would be a rough voyage home, that he had earned the enmity of Poseidon for blinding his son the Cyclops; he then went on to warn against eating the cattle of Helios the sun god that grazed on the island of Thrinacia.

Not only did Tiresias speak out strongly about the fatal disaster that lay ahead for the crew if they ate these cattle, but later, when they had sailed back to Circe's island for Elpenor's burial, she too in the firmest possible way warned Odysseus not to let his crew make a meal of the cattle of Helios. A rational person might find the warning strange, coming, as it did, from two persons whose probable omniscience makes clear that they knew perfectly well the outcome. Yet, on the other hand, one can say that this type of warning is entirely commonplace and obvious; there is the famous example of omniscient Yahweh forbidding Adam and Eve to eat the apple. Odysseus certainly literally knew what Tiresias and Circe had been saying, but somehow failed to consider that in the fairy-tale land through which they were traveling, prohibitions are introduced only to be violated. Cinderella, after all, ignored the clock hands moving toward midnight and went right on dancing. Perhaps Odysseus obsessed on telling the anecdote of the cattle of Thrinacia, so as to emphasize that his men destroyed *themselves* by their lack of discipline and patience, in contrast to himself, who accepted and endured the prohibition laid upon them.

Tiresias went on to say that Odysseus would find trouble at home, a house full of men courting his wife and wasting his estate in their daily food and wine consumption. Kill them was Tiresias' advice, then journey to where men do not know the sea—a tall order, it would seem, for someone living on an island in the Mediterranean. Over the Alps, perhaps, or into the Sahara. Go, said Tiresias, where men would mistake the function of an oar you carry over your shoulder, thinking it must have something to do with threshing. This is an imaginative way on Tiresias' part, one supposes, to point Odysseus in the direction of inland spaces with vast wheat fields, far away from a maritime economy. But, then you will come home, Tiresias continued, and die a peaceful death, not in war, but in well-fed, pampered old age. It will come from the sea, said Tiresias, adding nothing more precise ("from the sea" in the sense of *the sea as cause?* or "from the sea" in the sense of *at a distance from the sea?* Odysseus could not make up his mind), and he was gone, ceding his place to Anticleia.

When Odysseus' mother had drunk the blood and was animated to speak to her son, she went on immediately about the woes at Ithaca—the suitors in the house, the lengthy suffering of Penelope, who had to endure them there—and about old Laertes, who had withdrawn to the hills, and Telemachus, who administered the estates (surely so young as to be no more than a figurehead for people loyal to Odysseus, a mere formality to forestall any immediate claims to the throne that the suitors might make). Anticleia's gloomy account ended with words about her own death, true to a pattern of mothers to sons the world over, sparking, whether purposefully or no, monumental guilt: "It wasn't a heart attack that wasted me, dear son, nor had I a disease, no, I died broken hearted over you when you had been gone so long from me."

There at the Underworld entrance came the spirits of three comrades from the days of the Trojan War: Agamemnon, Achilles, and Ajax. After this encounter with them, Odysseus marveled at how they had carried their earthly personalities and concerns into the eternal murk where they were now passing the time.

Agamemnon was angry and bitter—what else?—this time over his murder, killed while a guest at the palace of Aegisthus, his wife's paramour "at a party, mind you!" Did Odysseus remember at that moment Agamemnon's involving him in the simulated wedding that had brought Iphigenia to Aulis, so that the father could sacrifice his daughter while the mother was helpless nearby? "She couldn't even shut my eyes and mouth, the slut, although I was dying," Agamemnon had continued. Whatever his feelings for the actors in this domestic drama, Odysseus would have found this breach of funereal etiquette and basic human respect odious and shocking. He might have been inwardly amused, however, at Agamemnon's attempt to portray himself as a victim when he tried to attach the death of Cassandra to his own: "There she was cut down next to me, I tried to raise myself up as she was dying." Cassandra's murder by Clytemnestra was a sad story, true enough, but somehow the "lord of men" forgot that it was he who had brought his sex slave home to Clytemnestra's house.

Agamemnon ended his diatribe with, "Beware of wives, Odysseus, they are always plotting against their husbands. You think of homecoming, the wife, the children, the welcoming slaves, and then there is the knife in your chest. She makes all women suspect."

He paused. "Not, of course, wise Penelope, the daughter of Icarius. She is entirely virtuous." The statement inspired him to another outburst against Clytemnestra and her refusal to let him see his son, even as he was dying. "Remember this, Odysseus. When you get to Ithaca, bring your ship in at some distant part of the island. Come up on her by surprise. You cannot trust women." Did indeed Odysseus ever wonder about his own wife, Penelope? He had just learned from Tiresias that she was beset by clamoring males who were suitors for her hand (her bed, really) and what was most important, *his* throne. Was she despairing of his ever returning, thinking her elderly father-in-law incompetent, her young son not yet capable of what needed doing? Odysseus had never voiced doubts about Penelope, but for the first time, he grew anxious about his return. His power was in jeopardy.

Achilles came forward in the company of Patroclus, his dear friend, and Nestor's son, Antilochus, while Ajax, the son of Telamon, remained off to the side. Seeing that company of great warriors reminded Odysseus of the glory days at Troy. He singled out Achilles to greet him warmly and remind him of his legendary stature among the Achaeans. He contrasted his own status as an aging vagrant, penniless, lost on the seas, despairing of finding his home, with Achilles, whose brilliant death on the field of battle, while youthful, beautiful, and in his prime, had ensured the integrity of his legend for all eternity, and given him pride of place among the souls in the Underworld. But Achilles, moody and bitter, exhibiting an attitude not much different from his self-centered point of view while alive, replied that he would rather be the meanest serf working the back acres of someone's farm on earth than king of the Underworld in death. There was no consolation for death. One wonders if Achilles' problem was not a failure to prepare for the retirement years, as they say nowadays, if that does not sound too facetious, when what is meant is its grandest, most transcendent meaning. He asked about his son then, and Odysseus was happy that he could report about the glory that had attached to Neoptolemus on the field at Troy when he took over his father's weapons—but shut his mind to that last scene in the palace at Troy that Queen Hecuba had described to him.

Odysseus then went over to Ajax, who was standing impassively nearby. The memory of Odysseus having been awarded the arms of Achilles with Ajax the loser, and the latter's subsequent suicide, was the breach between them. Odysseus immediately spoke of the contest, and his sorrow at the misery its outcome caused Ajax. He employed all his rhetorical skills to describe Ajax's lofty place among the Achaeans, how they grieved his absence from the field of battle after his death. The words altered nothing. Ajax turned away without speaking, and was gone.

There is no human curiosity greater than wonder at existence after death. Whole religions are founded or maintained on guaranteeing one or another notion of it. Few there are who can die once and return to tell the story, apart from those momentarily dead who describe the lights, the aura, the shimmer, and whatever other sensation akin to what the body intuits. Odysseus, however, got an extended glimpse of something else. He learned firsthand from the wandering dead soul of Elpenor that without a funeral, the rites, and the offerings, there can be no rest for a dead person, only perpetual wandering and displacement. For people of the Bronze Age, who lived directly from the land, nothing could have been more terrifying than being denied a resting place. Elpenor's plight was awful to them. Still, for the soul who has been properly taken care of, the body placed in a tomb, oil, food, and articles for living placed around him or her, there is not that much improvement; life after death, as Achilles' depression amply demonstrates, is gray, without substance, gloomy, and unsubstantial. The dead person is a wraith, animated and only partially incorporated when blood, the life-giving tonic, is drunk; that is perhaps the reason for the Achaeans' custom of pouring blood on the grave. Life after death seemed a place for humankind to regret, at least that is what Odysseus found among those he once knew. Yet there was also a place for some select few called the Elysian Fields. Here, as the tradition tells us, there is no snow, nor winter, nor rain, but instead a westerly breeze comes off Ocean that continually refreshes the souls who dwell there. As Menelaus never ceased to tell everyone, on his way home from Troy he was told by the old sea sprite Proteus that because he was married to Helen, and thus son-in-law of Zeus, he was one of the elect who after death would spend all eternity in the Elysian Fields. As ever, it's who you know, not what you do.

Having sailed back to Circe's island, Odysseus and his crew performed the burial rites for Elpenor of the broken neck, setting an oar into the mound of earth over his corpse as a marker. Odysseus had a chance to talk again with Circe, who gave him an extended itinerary of the experiences that lay before him. She told him that he must beware the enchantment of the Sirens' voices, that the whirlpool and riptides of Charybdis would require masterly captaining of the ships. ("How can I fight Charybdis?" "You can't fight a god, silly fool, just cut and run.") That the giant oceanic clutching arms of Scylla would be difficult to avoid (he would lose six men to Scylla). And, of course, she stressed the fatal prohibition against eating the cattle of Helios, which very shortly thereafter, with her warning words still presumably in their minds, the crew in defiance, fueled by their hunger, recklessly slaughtered and barbecued.

The event tells us something about Odysseus' command as well as his crew's attitude toward death and dying. They had been warned specifically and emphatically not to slaughter the cattle. To do so would mean their death. When the island came into view, Odysseus thought it better to put temptation out of reach by sailing on by, even though the failing light meant the onset of night. His sister's brother-in-law, Eurylochus, who was essentially second in command on the homeward journey, immediately put up a fuss. It was nighttime already, he complained, and they should beach the ship, not to mention that there might be a storm. Although it was Eurylochus' nature to cavil, his harsh remarks at that moment— "Odysseus has a heart of steel"—seem to have induced this leader of men to yield (or did he sense impending open mutiny?). "Just remember you are forcing me to it" was more or less Odysseus' response, and "I am only one among many," words that are difficult even to imagine him saying. He made them swear an oath that they would not touch the cattle. His trust seems utterly bizarre; fatigue must have beclouded his wits.

The next day dawned and there was no wind. As it turned out, they were becalmed a month, and supplies grew perilously low. Eurylochus began to grumble, to talk about taking the risk of eating the cattle, arguing that a quick death was better than the slow agony of dying of hunger. We do not know what Odysseus said to this. But again, quite uncharacteristically, Odysseus went off to the far end of the island, leaving the men behind. There he prayed to the gods, and fell asleep, as though prayer was his way of giving up control and sleep was the natural response. When he awoke and walked back to where they had pitched camp, he smelled beef cooking over coals. He cried out to the gods in rebuke that they let him sleep so that disaster could strike. He found the crew standing by their barbecue pit, each one blaming another for instigating the slaughter and cooking. To their horror, the skins of the flayed animals piled on the ground began to move, and the pieces of meat still on the spits began to low and bellow. That night they lay down to sleep sure of disaster, but the next day they woke up to a fair wind, so they set sail relatively cheerfully. For a brief moment it seemed as if they were going to get out safely, until with a giant crack the ship was split asunder by a bolt of lightning out of a cloudless blue sky.

The crew drowned, and Odysseus, the only one left alive, was alone, spinning along in the wide sea. Having climbed onto the keel, the long timber that ran from stem to stern, he was able to fashion a rude sailing vessel with a bit of mast still attached, and a piece of hide to catch the wind. A soft breeze sprang up driving him south until he was once more gliding near the dreaded Scylla and Charybdis. As he felt his boat being sucked down, he looked up and saw branches of a tall fig tree that grew precariously from the rocks above. These he grasped, suspending himself in air as his boat was sucked away into the whirlpool caused by the violent riptide meeting in the straits. He held on with all his might, hoping his strength would not desert him, until at last, just as Charybdis had sucked the boat in, so did she vomit it back up in a rising swell. Odysseus dropped down onto the wooden beam and paddled tortuously out of the whirlpool currents until he was in the calm of the sea and ready to get on his way if the wind would allow him. But where? For nine days he drifted over the sea as the winds took him until, on the tenth, he was washed up on the island of Ogygia, where lived the goddess Calypso.

CHAPTER 4

•◆•

LOVER

Wʜᴇɴ Oᴅʏssᴇᴜs ᴄᴀᴍᴇ to, he was no longer lying on the beach where he had the dimmest memory of a gently rolling surf depositing him. He was on soft bedding in the cave of Calypso, a nymph who dwelt on the island in the company of her female servants. She appeared to him to be a woman of early adulthood, yet mature, somehow ageless, something more easily sensed than explained; as he learned, she was, like Circe, outside of time. She too had a face of character and wisdom, yet one far more serene than Circe's. She was no witch—there were no sudden glints of unearthly wisdom or power piercing the soft glow that emanated from her deep-set dark eyes. Odysseus was too distracted by his predicament to notice much more about her. He wanted desperately to be off. Suddenly his yearning to return home had turned into uncontrollable craving.

Calypso seemed sympathetic, but she pointed out that there were no ships beached on her island, and in her experience no sailors ever passed that way. It was baffling. Ogygia, she told him, was the name of the island, but she had no sense at all of where it was in relation to any other place. The sun's rays told him which was north, south, east, and west, but Odysseus' repeated questions could not help Calypso to think where they were. She confessed that she had really never given the matter any consideration. Her father was Atlas, part of the generation of deities known as Titans who were overthrown by Zeus. Calypso, as far as she knew, had been from the beginning of time on Ogygia, perhaps exiled there; but she thought of herself as inborn to the nature of the place, its stones, its trees and grasses, winds, earth, sandy beaches, wavelets kissing the sand. She was Ogygia, her island. Now he was there, too; that was all there was to it. She was no witch, he kept telling himself; she wished him well, you could see that in her smile. She just didn't share his urgency.

At first he was too weak to stand. Calypso was always at his side, regulating his water, his diet, even helping him eliminate, although he could see, dim as his eyesight was, that there were serving girls aplenty to perform these tasks. He was shivering, even though she had placed him close to the hearth, where cedar and citron wood burned, giving off every now and then a slight puff of a back draft; its pungent, almost sweet aroma obliterated the dank, acrid smell of a sick, tired, dirty male. Days passed and he was sitting in a chair opposite her, eating some meat served on bronze plates of exotic design, drinking sweet wine mixed with water, looking up from his food to see her unswerving gaze upon him, a steady observation of his person that, he now had begun to perceive, had started when first he opened his eyes the day of his deliverance. They had yet to speak of anything beyond the exigencies of his situation, except that in response to his curious glance, she indicated that her cup contained nectar and her plate held ambrosia.

Calypso's gaze was so unrelenting that Odysseus felt ashamed to do more than snatch quick glances at her full, firm breasts, her shapely legs that supported her long torso. She was slender, remarkably tall, more slender and tall than Circe. Maybe it was her hair that hung straight, framing her face and spilling down beyond her shoulders that made her seem so tall. The set of her face was stern, almost scowling when she looked at him from deep within her dark brown eyes, which seemed almost black at times. He could not read them easily. Calypso, he had to admit, made him uneasy. Once he felt steady enough to walk about on his own, he went away from the cave down to the beach, as much to put distance between himself and his formidable hostess as to pray to Athena for deliverance.

Whenever he emerged from the entrance to the cave, he never ceased to rejoice at the sight. Climbing around the entrance was a grapevine thick with shade-giving leaves and hanging low with large bunches of grapes. He walked through a grove of trees—alder, black poplar, and fragrant cypress—which had been planted there as a kind of windbreak for the cave entrance. The trees were haven to all kinds of seafaring birds who soared out and over the sea by day; at night he could hear the owls hoot from the branches. The sounds of the twittering creatures mingled with the delicious rustle of softly running water. This came from springs that fed four fountains, each falling into a channel sending the water in a different direction. Beyond were lush green meadows deep green with parsley, dotted with clusters of purple and white violets. He recalled the orchards of his childhood in Ithaca, the long rows of fruit trees and vines his father tended so faithfully, and the longing to see them again set him to crying.

He walked forth from the cave every morning. No sooner was he a little way down the path than he could hear Calypso singing over the clicking sound made by the shuttle as she started to weave at the immense loom that stood in one corner of the cave. Day after day, it was the same thing, he could hear Calypso in the cave singing as he left and upon his return. That was how it had been with Circe, too. The mystery of it was that they both stopped the minute they sensed his presence, stopped singing, stopped weaving. It chilled him at times to realize how elusive they were. Calypso did a prodigious amount of weaving. The fabric lay on a table in the center room where her attendants could go to it when they wanted to stitch up pieces of clothing. When it was sunny and warm the girls sat in a row before the cave sewing. More than once they ran up to him upon his return to hold an unfinished cloak up against his body; soon he had to tell them that he had more clothes than he could ever wear. It made him uneasy watching them stitch up so many items for him, as though he would never be able to leave, as though somehow they knew this to be true.

He was not always free to walk forth as he chose. When he had recovered, Calypso directed him to the fields nearby and asked him to apply his man's strength to tilling the soil. It was an odd experience to be the only man on the island, at least that was what seemed to be the case, odder still to do fieldwork, which in his entire life had been the task of peasants. He plowed with a yoke of oxen and the girls followed with their skirts held out filled with seed, which they cast into the furrows. When it was time to harvest, he soon learned the rhythmic movement of the body as he used a sickle to cut the wheat, while the taller girls followed him, tying the sheaves, and the smaller girls gathered them up. Calypso led her favorite farm cattle out to trample the grain as it was threshed from the ears; round they went on the hard-beaten earth. Then it was time to winnow, throwing the crushed ears into the wind with a wooden paddle that resembled a shovel, watching the grain fall to the ground as the chaff blew away in the wind. When the sheep hair was long Odysseus sheared it off, and it went into baskets to be processed into yarn by the spinners. Other times he pruned the various fruit trees—pear, pomegranate, apple, and fig. Because they all blossomed at different times of year, there was always a harvest for the girls to pluck from the branches. On the hills there were olive trees and terraces of vineyards, ripening sometimes for raisins, sometimes for wine. The grapes that the girls had picked for raisins he set out in the sun on giant wooden trays covered with a delicate gauzelike fabric so that the birds would not get at them.

In the late fall, when there was a distinct chill in the air, all the girls, Calypso, and Odysseus went through the groves of olive trees carrying a large linen cloth, sewn together from many pieces Calypso had made on her loom. Demeter's peplos, the girls called it, a cloth that they set under each olive tree in succession. Then they shook the branches, everyone taking the branch that fit their height, sometimes standing in the crotch of the tree, and the ripe olives rained down on the cloth. Again and again they carried the loaded cloth to the shed for the olive pressings. After the pressing there would be the ravishing taste of fresh olive oil for their bread. Odysseus discovered a pleasure he never known, only experienced secondhand as a child: the satisfaction of knowing that the storage granaries were filled for another season. He grew brown again, his only covering against the sun being the loincloth at his hips. Often when he stood at the completion of a task as the heat of the day came upon them, Calypso appeared with a towel to dry the sweat from his chest, holding out to him a goblet containing a concoction of wine, honey, grated cheese, and barley. He thought back to his time with Circe, wondering that he had never noticed how the work got done. What had she done all day? What had he done all day? All he remembered was the sexual excitement, and thought that this was probably what it meant to have lived with a witch. It had all been so mysterious.

Calypso had a life of tasks, he saw: she was forever organizing her girls to deal with the clothes, washing them, arranging them on the shelves; or she was directing the girls in collecting food, preparing, and cooking it for their daily meals; and at other times she was turning clay on the wheel, making vases, cups, and plates, which she then painted. In all her activities she was instructing her attendants, who seemed to be eternally new at the job, young, and extraordinarily vivacious. Their favorite pastime when not working was to sit on an embroidered cloth with Calypso out under the trees and go through her jewelry boxes, shrieking with laughter at the effects achieved with the various arrangements of gems on their arms, legs, ears, fingers, and around their necks and on their heads.

As he was soon to discover, Calypso was not shy about showing her sexual desire for him. She had found Odysseus near death, nursed him back to health, all the while handling his body with the tenderest care, feeding him, bathing him, very gently massaging healing unguents into the numerous deep cuts he had sustained on his rough, tumbling ride through the surf onto the rocks of her beach. But there came a time when he wanted to take over from his nurse to manage on his own. One day while he sat in a large copper tub, immersed in steaming water, as she ran the sponge down his back he suddenly asked to use it himself, perhaps a little abruptly, a little rudely—he sensed it instantly—but she made no comment. She yielded the sponge, and then, as he sponged his face and squeezed water over his head, she reached into the water and began ever so gently to run her hands over his entire body.

It had been some time since his days and nights with Circe.

He was excited as Calypso took his hand and pulled him up from the water, rubbed him dry, and led him off to the large bed she maintained for herself in a kind of grotto off the main area of the cave. He had his strength back; lust fueled his performance into the small hours of the night. It was the first time since his arrival that he felt that he was making contact with this strange woman. He assumed that their lovemaking after the bath presaged a new intimacy. Calypso, it seemed, had other ideas. He and Circe had fought a duel, they had negotiated, made a pact, and their lovemaking sprang from that mutual understanding. He remained unsure of Calypso. She would be there waiting to put him into her bed, use him, that was how he felt it, just as she sometimes took up her skein of wool, broke off a piece with her long, elegant fingers, threaded it through her shining needle, and began sewing. It was stuff for her creations, just like the cedar wood kindled the flames. That was how he saw himself in Calypso's bed.

On that first occasion when they awoke, the sun had already moved up into the sky. He was only half awake, and for a moment the stiffness and ache in his thighs from the lovemaking returned him to the days of the shipwreck; yet in an instant, his memory of the night before transformed it into a good feeling. When he sat at the table across from Calypso, servants handed him cheese and bread. She looked at him attentively, but said nothing. Shortly, he left for his usual perambulation of the island, which would take him eventually to a rise of rock near the southern shore, where he spent so many of his days scanning the horizon, straining his eyes to detect a sail. He remained a castaway, that he knew. All the while, as he looked out, tears ran down his cheeks as he thought of his father growing old without him, of his son living in a house without a father, of the fields and cattle cared for by slaves without any sure direction. When he thought of his wife, Penelope, it was to worry that she would not have the strength to withstand the suitors.

As the winter season brought shorter days, Odysseus and Calypso spent more time in bed. There was nothing else to do when the sunlight brought the day to a close; the firelight was not sufficient for whittling new farm utensils or furniture pieces, sewing, or any other task that Odysseus had dreamt up to stave off the utter boredom of his life. Calypso responded instantly to his physical presence in the bed; she was easily aroused.

There came a day, however, when Odysseus returned from his southside perch sunk in depression. It had dawned on him that for almost what he guessed was half a year—that is how he read the path of the sun, in any case—his anxiously scanning eyes had sighted nothing on the seas. The realization brought a weight down upon his shoulders, he sagged miserably, quickly tired, as though he had been hauling rocks for hours, even days. That night when he lay beside Calypso, she was surprised at his unresponsiveness; it seemed that nothing would rouse him from the gloom and torpor of his depression. At last she managed to get him to perform, after which he rolled over almost immediately. She said nothing but, just before they fell into their separate dream paths of sleep, she looked at him perplexed.

The following nights were new territory for Odysseus, who thought he had wandered through all the marvels and oddities of the world up to this point. Calypso devised new sexual games and positions night after night in her determination to keep Odysseus interested. They made love on the floor, on the table, in the copper bath, again in the bath with the servant girls pouring warm water over them. At first Odysseus was shy before the spectators until he mastered the erotic potential of an audience. The next event was when one of the women joined them in the bed, complicating and invigorating their sexual couplings. He was surprised to see how amorous the two women were with each other, but, as he thought it over, he understood how he was the variant on the norm in the thousands of nights on that island.

But then as these routines inevitably settled into just that—routines—it became boring, the old problem, really, of mistaking the dance for the dancer. The two of them made an unspoken pact: she wanted his lovemaking, he would do his duty. Nights after their dinner they mounted the bed, lay deep in the sweet-smelling sheets, always freshly washed and dried in the brilliant, cleansing sunlight, and they made love.

And so it went year after year. It wasn't bad, but after five years he was having an increasingly difficult time doing it. It was a job, he realized, just like those performed by all the menials in his palace in Ithaca. He hardened his heart as he hardened himself and kept on going. If he could endure the din and terror of battle for ten long years, storms at sea, if he could tenaciously keep his hold on a piece of broken drifting mast, not let go and sink to the depths, he could manage to pleasure Calypso nightly. Once in a great while, when his mind strayed from the job at hand, he thought back to those first days with Penelope when every act of love carried the association of baby-making. He considered it odd that neither Circe nor Calypso mentioned babies, nor became pregnant. Years later, when he thought of them, he decided that immortal women living as they did on those islands did not want the continuum of eternal time ruptured by a new life coming into being.

With the approach of the sixth summer, as the days grew longer the hours of daylight after dinner stretched out uncomfortably for Odysseus, who now had no energy or desire for marathon sexual evenings. He sensed that Calypso shared his boredom, watching her dawdle over her plate and goblet, as though she were trying to prolong the meal in some magical way until bedtime. One night he broke the silence with an anecdote about his years at Troy. Something about the bronze dinner plates on which they were served their food reminded him in a flash of similar ones—the same pattern, really, same thickness of metal, an entire set that fell to his lot following a raid upon one of the neighboring people in the hills behind Troy. To his surprise, as he began his narrative, he felt himself falling into a kind of singsong pattern and he realized that he was mimicking the song language the court poets employed.

Agamemnon had brought his favorite poet from Mycenae, whose nightly job was to sing to him and to all the leaders who gathered about in his tent. Every night the old fellow told of Agamemnon's royal lineage, of his family's descent from Zeus, of the exploits of his ancestors; at other times, he recounted episodes from battles: cattle rustling, cities besieged, ships at sail. He had quite a repertory of stories to sing, and sometimes he seemed to update them, fitting out events to match the plains of Troy, the river Scamander, for instance, or the battlements of the city, and even, when he grew inspired, introducing some of the local actors, Hector, or Paris. Some of the younger men knew how to recite the old stories in the proper rhythm. It required a lot of memory work, setting the words to the units of lengths, some syllables needing to be held longer, some shorter, and of course having that great storehouse of formulae, words, phrases, story lines, and characters at the ready in the brain. Performing was quite intricate, but there was so much repetition that if one had heard it from childhood on, it was not impossible to master, at least as a rank amateur with pauses, delays, and misspoken words. Odysseus had heard Achilles do the singing quite well, taking turns with Patroclus; they were both excellent perform-ers. It was what some of the more cultured young aristocrats aspired to. Odysseus had always been quite impressed.

His narration now was almost instinctive. Once Odysseus started reciting for Calypso, the old stories, the language, and the rhythm began to coalesce into something with discernible narrative shape. Within a month or so, he had it together enough to embark upon casting details of his own experiences into the formulae and stereotypes thrown up from his memory of song. His childhood adventures, the grim days in battle at Troy, the strange terrors and oddities of his sea voyage through the Mediterranean when he had been blown off course, became recast into the traditional story line. Any battle became the war at Troy, any storm at sea became those in which he struggled for his life, fairy tales became the ogres and witches who confronted him, everyman became Odysseus. Calypso sat rapt, idly twisting a strand of her long hair between her fingers and staring at him as she had always done, in total silence. The serv-ing women came in from their quarters, crouching on the floor. As the daylight waned and night came on, Odysseus found himself looking into ten pairs of eyes, lit up and shining in the gloom, reflecting back to him the flickering flames of the fire.

He had managed more or less to accept this somewhat coma-tose existence as one that would serve him until he uttered his last breath, when suddenly it all changed. One day, Calypso came down to find him at his perch, where he still sat so often scanning the sea. He could hear her crashing through the underbrush long before he saw her. She was panting, her normally sallow cheeks had two burn-ing red patches on them, her mouth was twisted in an angry grimace. Quite inexplicably she began a tirade—it was more than he had ever heard her say in all the time he had spent on Ogygia—all about the male chauvinism of the gods on Mount Olympus, how the male gods were allowed to have all the mortal females they might want for sexual partners, but when any of the female divinities started to do the same thing and get a man, a human, for a sexual partner, they were stopped. One disaster or another would fell the chosen male. Or even worse, she screamed, telling him what happened to the poor goddess of the dawn. Dawn, it seemed, got herself a mortal named Tithonus and then somehow endowed him with immortality, but forgot, or more likely the male gods made her forget, to give him eternal youth, so there she was to the end of time with this complete vegetable pissing and shitting and puking in their—what she thought would be—love nest.

Odysseus realized what had fueled this strange outburst when she turned to him, grasped his shoulders, and angrily told him that the god Hermes had just visited her with the news that Zeus had ordered her to send Odysseus on his way home. Athena, it seemed, had pled with her father, who had finally yielded. It was a perfect moment, Hermes had explained, because Poseidon, who hated Odysseus, was off on the southern rim of the globe visiting the Ethiopians, who were holding a festival in his honor. The storms that bedeviled Odysseus had sprung from the implacable hostility of Poseidon, a father's revenge for the blinding of his son, the Cyclops. Zeus, on the other hand, was willing to do this favor for his daughter Athena, because he too loved Odysseus. Hermes had explained to Calypso, who in turn related the facts to Odysseus, that when his crew had so foolishly eaten the cattle of Helios on Thrinacia, Lampetia, the nymph daughter of Helios, who tended the cattle of Thrinacia, made a special prayer to her father. He in turn went in supplication to Zeus, and as Odysseus' ship sailed away from the island, the father of men and gods, as Zeus was called, sent a thunderbolt that rent the ship asunder. But that was a very special circumstance, and in the end Odysseus had come out of it alive.

Now Calypso insisted all would be well. Zeus had promised him a safe voyage home, and Hermes had told Calypso to help Odysseus build some kind of boat for his trip. Odysseus looked out over the endless expanse of ocean and shuddered. He asked Calypso to swear that she would help him, that she was not plotting any trickery. His suspicious nature and demands for oaths delighted Calypso. She smiled and patted his hand, assuring him that she meant him well and would swear the required oath. Anyway, as she added, if Zeus could split a ship in two and drown Odysseus' crew, he could as easily endow any craft, whatever it was they might build, with the capacity, however supernatural it might seem, to survive any conceivable storm at sea.

That evening they had their usual meal, except that Calypso sent the women away, placed Odysseus in the very throne in which she usually sat, and served him herself. After she herself was seated, Calypso sulkily remarked that she was sure that Penelope could hardly rival her when it came to lovemaking. She then, in what was obviously the last chip to be played, offered Odysseus immortality if he would stay there with her. She faced him across the table, silent after that, eyes by turns downcast or sparkling in rage, then dulled in petulance, even shedding the occasional tear. He had eaten in silence, head down facing his food, only every now and then glancing at this unfolding emotional tempest, pondering the horror of spending eternity on this island. Life was to be lived, his instinct was to go on to new things; perhaps those years of traveling had habituated him to change, but no, change was inherent in the human condition, death was another experience, as much a part of life as birth. Death provides the dimension for life; without it choice has no meaning. It suddenly came to him that Tithonus, whom Calypso had described as having been made immortal but not eternally young, could be a metaphor for the only possible human experience of immortality. In one way or another a human being made immortal would become a vegetable because it is the very essence of the human being to be dying from the day of birth; take that awareness away and there is nothing essential left. Take that away and they are zombies, mush, no edge to their consciousness, no depth to their thinking.

When he had finished his food, Odysseus had had time to think of a diplomatic reply: that indeed Penelope could hardly equal Calypso when it came to a great body, beautiful face, sexual charms, erotic technique. As for the gift of immortality, he thanked her but declined. He wanted to get home, he explained, to see his son, his lands, his father. Calypso treated this rejection with the same equanimity Circe had displayed. They went to bed and the prospect of his imminent escape gave Odysseus the high-hearted gusto to fulfill his erotic duties with a flourish that completely satisfied Calypso for the first time in years.

Much, much later, whenever he thought of that evening, Calypso's offer, and his refusal, he realized that the contrast between those thirteen years of warfare and then travel and the seven years of domestic routine were far more dramatic than he had credited them. His younger days had been too exciting for him to accept the life on Ogygia. He reviewed it all, the excitement of battle, the manipulation of his fellow officers, the triumph in winning the battle and surviving the war, the constant pulse-pounding horrors of the wandering years, the anxiety in those strange encounters, those extraordinary deviations from the norm, the triumph of enduring them all, and surviving. Circe had been a personal revelation to him: he had never known his capacity as a sexual person. Calypso presented a greater challenge. The quotidian sameness—which at first had soothed him, allowed him the space to enact the rituals of creating life, in the sex, in the farming—finally repelled him, he knew that all too well now. (Reviewing these years when he was a very old man, Odysseus recognized that there was in that moment in Ogygia only one constant upon which he could fasten his sights—his son, Telemachus, back in Ithaca. What he did not understand, however, is that he seemed not to have been able to form any serious attachment to another person. What about the son? the reader might ask. But yearning for his son, it could be argued, is much more of a narcissistic impulse than anything else.)

The next morning Calypso gave Odysseus an axe and led him to a stand of alder, pine, and poplar that had long ago died and dried out, perfect for something that needed to float. He felled twenty of these and trimmed them into planks with an adze, also provided by Calypso. She then returned with an auger—strange how many building tools she had about the place, he thought in retrospect, and how he had never noticed them before—and he bored holes through the boards, inserting dowels and binding them together with cords. He next built rudimentary sides, so that he had constructed a floating box, more than a raft, and made a raised deck after flooring the twenty long logs, and stuffing packing into the joins to keep the water out. His sewing skills came in handy when Calypso brought down fabric for the sails. He made a mast and fastened the sails to it.

Four days had passed. All was ready. That night, Odysseus, although tired from his shipbuilding exertions, again performed brilliantly to give Calypso an appropriate erotic finale to their seven years together in bed.

At last the moment arrived for departure. Calypso furnished

him with a skin filled with wine, another full of sweet water, and a bag of provisions. She said Hermes had told her that he was to sail straight, keeping his eye on the Pleiades and the Big Dipper on his right. Calypso promised to give him a favorable sea breeze and with a kiss sent him off. Seven years of his life, the longest relationship he had ever known, came to an end. Odysseus did not look back.

Seventeen days of smooth sailing gave him confidence and when he sighted a land mass directly before him, his heart leaped. As he realized in retrospect, those happy days should have filled him with suspicion; Poseidon would not let him go so easily and, as to the report that the god was at a celebration with the Ethiopians, the hope of his staying long with those distant people was illusory. Indeed, the skies darkened as a storm blew up. There was a sudden shrilling hurricane of contrary winds that collided, snapped off the mast, and ripped Odysseus from the boat into the water. Swimming desperately, spitting out the salt water, he managed to regain the shell as it turned round and round like a piece of bark in the eddies of a swift-running stream. Struggling over the side, he lay in the bottom, determined to hold on to the shell of the boat, when another wind, lashing giant waves, struck him. He would have drowned then if a sea nymph named Ino had not taken pity on him. Swooping down in the form of a gannet, the large web-footed bird of the sea, she perched on the gunwale and offered him her magical veil. She told him to strip off his clothes, wrap the veil around his chest, and swim as hard as he could for the nearby island of Scheria; with that she flew away. Bewildered and half-drowned as he was, his instinctive suspicion kept him from doing what she told him, at least for some moments while he pondered. Then another giant wave knocked him under, making him desperate for breath. He jettisoned the new clothes Calypso had made for him, and wrapped the veil about his chest. Another great blast suddenly rent his boat into bits, leaving him with only one plank, to which he clung desperately.

For two days the veil held him like a life jacket, while at first he floated; a pounding surf almost dashed him against the rocks, jagged bits of a shore that he had seen earlier from the calm seas. He paddled with all his might parallel to this menace until he sensed sweet water in the midst of the salt. A river! He swam hard, calling out in prayer to the river god, who was not under the jurisdiction of Poseidon, lord of the sea, asking for a calm passage into the shore. He lifted his head over the waves, which were calmer suddenly, peering through the gloom of the descending evening, and positioned himself so that he could swim into the river, the waters of which were mingling with the salty sea. At last he brought himself wearily up on the sand. After some moments of confusion his analytical mind took over: he would perhaps become dangerously cold if he stayed naked on the beach, but if he went to the hills, animals might attack him while he slept. In the growing darkness he could just make out a hollow nearby, a declivity filled with the leaves cast off by trees leaning drunkenly above it and from its sides. Heaping these together mechanically in a stupor of fatigue, he dropped down and instantly fell asleep.

It seemed to Odysseus only moments later that he was being wrenched from his sleep, jerked awake by shrill cries. His eyes opened to daylight, which, when he turned his head cautiously to gaze up, he gauged to be the bright light of midday. As the cries persisted, he groaned, wondering what kind of people he had come among. Then gradually he realized that the cries were the cries of girls at play—he heard laughing and giggles amid the shrieks. He rose, hidden from view by the drop in the ground where he had slept, peered out through the surrounding trees and bushes and saw them, twelve girls, about sixteen years old, quite beautiful he was quick to note, although the salt caking his eyelashes somewhat obscured his vision. They were gathered about in a circle awaiting the toss of a ball held high by one of them who, he decided, was a princess. Her clothing told him nothing; they all were dressed in the same kind of simple, diaphanous material that covered their bodies to the knee. It was her superior physical beauty, her commanding manner, and most of all the deference of the other girls, which was easy to recognize. She held the ball high, and he saw her little breasts through the thin fabric of her gown. He stumbled forward, desperate for humanity and assistance, with just enough forethought to break off a leafy frond to cover his penis.

At the sight of him, the girls fled screaming, except the very one he had especially noticed. The princess stood her ground, a little forlorn looking, apprehensive, very much alone, her shoulders slightly hunched together as though she expected a giant blow to be dealt her out of the sky. Still, she tossed her head back like a spirited colt and looked firmly at him as he approached her, stumbling with fatigue, trying to recover the equilibrium of walking on land after so many days being tossed about in the sea. He held the branch in his hand tightly in place, not even daring to glance down to assure himself that it was covering adequately, judging instead from the feel of the leaves that scratched his crotch while he walked. When he was a few feet from her, he paused and pondered. The custom of supplication was to kneel at the feet of a person and grasp their knees. Odysseus knew he could not drop his branch, he could not let his dirty, salty body touch the skin of that delicate creature; he was unsure what would happen if he felt a girl's soft body through his fingertips. He stood therefore at this slight distance and begged assistance, using the kind of language that he knew so well, comparing her with Artemis, the virgin goddess of nature, saying that perhaps indeed she was Artemis herself, and he should therefore be addressing prayers to her. He concluded with a compliment for the man who would take so lovely a creature as his wife. It was perhaps a forward and somewhat insinuating remark for a naked male to make to a nubile young girl girl standing before him. Certainly it was calculated.

The girl flushed. He marveled at the perfect structure of her face, the soft blush on her cheeks coming through the dusky hue of her skin. Her eyelashes, which she lowered modestly whenever she remembered that she was speaking to a stranger, were long and very black, framing deep, serious eyes that looked at him honestly. Her pink lips were as full and soft as the nose above was long, strong, and almost without a bridge. It was an arrogant nose, the nose of power and authority.

There was no trace of shyness, nor was the girl insecure; she knew the drill. She spoke out commandingly as much to the girls as to Odysseus, as though she were on the porch of her parents' palace. Strangers are sacred to Zeus, he protects suppliants, she observed, as she welcomed Odysseus. She spoke forcefully and loudly to him, and identified herself as Nausicaa, daughter of the king, whose name was Alcinous. The island was called Scheria; its people were Phaeaceans, and they were ruled by twelve kings, along with Alcinous, the thirteenth and most powerful, their superior. Today had been washing day, she explained. Her brothers' clothes were dirty, she had asked her father to have a cart hitched up, and she and her girls had brought the garments to the washing basins at the river's mouth, stamping them with their feet in the shallow water, setting them out on the sand to dry. By now having recovered herself completely, she offered to have one of her attendants wash him in the softly running water of one of the river's streams; but Odysseus, although he knew it was the normal custom of hospitality, felt strangely vulnerable in his nakedness and chose to go apart to wash himself, then wind himself into a loincloth and slip over it a chiton, both of which Nausicaa had selected from the pile of neatly folded clothes that the girls were preparing for the return journey in the cart.

When he returned, freshly bathed, something had happened, he could sense it. He felt that he glowed with good health and vigor, that something more than a good bath and an oiling had transformed him. He could see it in Nausicaa's appraising eyes, desiring him, she a girl of perhaps sixteen, he a man approaching fifty. Thank you, Athena, he muttered softly to himself, for making my way easier here. After he had eaten a bit from the remains in their picnic basket, Nausicaa told him that he must go to the city, to her parents' palace, to supplicate the queen. Nausicaa was emphatic on this. He was to pass by the king when he entered the throne room, go directly to the queen, and ask her aid. If she took an interest in his case, said Nausicaa, all would be well.

With another of her delightful blushes, which aroused Odysseus more than he would have imagined—perhaps, he decided, it was because Circe and Calypso being nymphs, and thus immortal, did not have blushes in their repertory—she insisted that he wait enough time to give her and her girls the chance to reach the city before he set out for the palace. The road was deserted where they were standing, she pointed out, but closer to the city there would be people. She did not want—oh, the blushes kept coming and were so charming—did not want, she was slightly stammering, that the gossips of the town think she had found some boyfriend from off island, when it was known only too well how boring and loutish she thought all the local boys were. So Odysseus would have to make his way alone on the road into town and into the palace. And off she went, girls, cart, and all, up the road to the town, leaving Odysseus to think over how Nausicaa had been as calculated in her remarks as he. At last he had met a woman who knew how to use language; how amusing it was, how tantalizing.

He looked after the dust swirls on the road made by the departing cart, through which the glistening golden hair of the girl holding the reins was barely visible. He was surprised at his interest in her; sentimental it was, yearning, tender, almost embarrassing. A girl, of course; he had not been around a girl for twenty years, as he thought of it. A silly fantasy spun into his head, whirled about like a top, making him just the least bit dizzy: Nausicaa, the young girl bride, gazing up at him, while he, the gray-haired groom, smiled down at her, taking in her gently heaving child's breasts as well as her shy, inviting smile, as he slowly lowered himself onto her girlish body. Circe and Calypso had changed him. He reveled in the fantasy, anticipating Nausicaa as the next great adventure, forgetting for an instant that he wanted to get home.

Odysseus made his way up the road, keeping his eye on the men he saw at a distance ahead of him. He had been prepared for the rough encounters a strange male must always expect from the locals when coming into their territory. When none of the men he passed seemed to notice him, he gradually realized that he was invisible, sensed that he was looking through a scrim, covered over in a mist. It must have been another of the careful strategies of security devised for him by Athena. The road came next to a grove of poplar trees, from which a spring gushed out into a meadow that surrounded it. This was a grove sacred to Athena, Nausicaa had told him, where he was to wait until enough time had passed for her to reach home. The shade, which dramatically lowered the temperature of the air of the late afternoon sun's heat, enveloped him, and gave him the presence of the goddess. He prayed to Athena, thanking her for the mist and for his reception from the young princess, and supplicated the goddess for help in getting home to Ithaca, hoping that these people would find him transportation.

He then went out again onto the road, which soon brought him to the beginnings of a city whose grand buildings set him gawking in amazement. He was so awestruck that he was startled suddenly to encounter standing on the road before him a young girl, who was looking at him intently. She apparently had no trouble penetrating the mist that obscured him to others. Her abrupt appearance, something about her manner, a certain audacious sense of control and authority, told him he was in the presence of Athena in disguise. He decided to trust his intuition and risk speaking in public to so young a female. When the girl offered to lead him to the palace, he was certain it was Athena, who was yet again, he realized, determined to create the perfect circumstance for his arrival.

The girl gave him background information as they walked along: Alcinous was the grandson of Poseidon who had made love to Periboa, the daughter of Eurymedon; from this union sprang Nausithous who in turn begat Alcinous and Rhexenor; when his brother, Rhexenor, died leaving only female issue, a daughter named Arete, Alcinous married her, his own niece. The girl then pointed ahead to a most extraordinary palace in which the royal family lived. As Odysseus entered and began to walk through it, he knew that it was something he had never seen before, not at Troy, not at Mycenae. The walls were bronze, the frieze cobalt, the doors gold, the pillars silver. Torches held by sculptured forms of young men, made of gold, illuminated the interior passageways. Outside, as Odysseus could see from the porch, were orchards of every kind of fruit—pears, apples, figs—alongside which stretched rows of vines heavy with grapes. In vast kitchen gardens grew a variety of vegetables, each kind standing in neat squares outlined by boxwood hedges. The entire area was watered by an elaborate irrigation system, which kept the vegetation exceedingly lush.

Odysseus entered the palace unchallenged by the men standing on the porch and in the adjacent corridor. The mist, he realized, must still cover him. He walked along the corridor, which he decided must lead to the throne room, until suddenly he was there, standing on an immense polished threshold stone. Athena must have dissipated the mist at his entry because the crowd in the room stared in his direction in surprised silence. He walked on in, straight to Arete, the woman so obviously the queen, mother of the imperious girl who had welcomed him on the beach. Kneeling before her and clasping her knees, he begged her for haven in the palace, and prayed that she and her court would devise a way for him to get home to his native land. With that he moved aside to sit down at the edge of the hearth almost in the ashes. The people in the room remained deep in silence.

Finally an old man, Echeneos (as Odysseus was to learn later), spoke out, chiding Alcinous for not raising Odysseus from his suppliant position, giving him a chair, and getting a serving woman to bring out some food. Echeneos repeated the sentiments Nausicaa had expressed at the beach about Zeus' protection of the suppliant, the sanctity of the suppliant, and then proposed a toast to Zeus, who honored suppliants. That seemed to jolt Alcinous into instant action; he clapped his hands and shouted through a door immediately at his side, and within minutes a maidservant brought in a tray heaped with food, and wine was poured liberally all around for a toast to Zeus. Then the king, in dismissing the court, as Odysseus listened in shock at the suddenness of it all, urged his courtiers to devise strategies for getting the stranger home to his family. Odysseus found it curious that Alcinous also publicly expressed the hope that the stranger were not some god come down to earth to test the piety of the Phaeaceans, adding that before they had always come openly. No, no, Odysseus had responded, chuckling softly, no god, just a long-suffering human, hoping to eat a little dinner, and then get help finding a way home. I'll be content to die, Odysseus declared in a ringing voice, once I have seen my property, my people who work my land, and my house. (Readers will note that here as elsewhere Odysseus has no thought for his wife, Penelope, an omission that seems curious today, but is rather much in keeping for a patriarchal male of that period. Of course, it could be argued that a male of this period did not make public reference to a wife, or perhaps Odysseus— still under the spell of meeting Nausicaa—was not up to reminding himself of his marital bonds.)

The room emptied out, leaving the three of them—Odysseus, Alcinous, and Arete—in silence. Odysseus was enjoying another plate of choice bits of meat and vegetables specially brought in for him by the maidservant, when Arete spoke out in a high, clear voice asking him where he had acquired the clothes he was wearing. She recognized the pieces as belonging to her sons, she noted, as though to apologize for the tactlessness so direct a question implied. Who are you, she added, thereby violating the ritual of hospitality that demands that questions of identity be delayed until appropriate food, drink, and rest have been offered to the stranger. Odysseus, however, had no intention of answering with his name, so he narrated instead the story of his travails in the sea, his encounter with Calypso, concluding with a description of his meeting Nausicaa on the beach who, he said, was so very kind to provide him with clothing and something to eat. To his surprise, the mild-mannered Alcinous was severe in criticizing Nausicaa for not bringing him to her parents, as she was the first to receive him as a suppliant. Odysseus quickly lied to protect the girl, saying she had of course wanted to do so, but he had stopped her because he was afraid that her parents would be angry with her for coming home with a stranger in tow.

Alcinous vigorously shook his head, almost shouting out that he and Arete were not like that. Then—and for as long as he lived Odysseus would never forget this moment—after a brief silence, the king fixed Odysseus with a serious look, and confessed that he would be most pleased to see the stranger stay on to become his son-in-law. Odysseus never forgot the rush of emotion that overtook him as he heard Alcinous' words, the intoxication of longing to accept the king's invitation, settle his life, stop the wandering, begin again, lose himself in a teenage girl's fragrant and fresh body—a girl who furthermore had given every indication of being besotted with him on first view, ready to serve him, follow where he led. He scarcely heard Alcinous adding that he would endow him with riches and property as well as his daughter; but that if the stranger wanted to go home, wanted to see again his homeland, his house, and whatever else might be close to his heart, then he would order a ship out the next day to sail him home no matter how far that might be. At the last of the king's remarks, Odysseus came to; his mind was made up by the second proposition, so he publicly uttered a prayer to Zeus that Alcinous do as he had promised and get him home to his own country. With that Arete motioned to some women servants and ordered a bed to be made up for Odysseus in one of the porticoes. Within minutes, she and Alcinous had retired to their chambers, and Odysseus was asleep in his bed on the marble floor of the portico.

Next morning Alcinous called an assembly of the leading Phaeaceans. His proposal that fifty young men be charged with making one of their ships ready to transport the stranger home was enthusiastically approved. Then Alcinous invited them all to a midday feast in the open courtyard in front of the palace where he had ordered a blind singer named Demodocus to provide entertainment. As it happened, the singer chose to sing episodes of the war at Troy, certainly the subject du jour for oral poets. He sang of a quarrel between Odysseus and Achilles, which, as Demodocus described it, pleased Agamemnon because an oracle from Delphi had declared that the war against Troy would be won only when these two fell out. At first Odysseus was vastly amused and maybe a little irritated at the way in which this poet had taken a well-known incident, the quarrel between Achilles and Agamemnon, and converted it to new purposes. Demodocus was using the language and style of the traditional narratives, a poetic manner that insisted upon its own verisimilitude, if not indeed absolute fidelity to historical fact. Odysseus was sympathetic to a poet's propensity for embellishment and alteration of traditional material. In any case, who knew how Demodocus had received his material and where or when this perversion of events had entered the canon? He knew that he had manipulated mightily himself when describing the Trojan War to Calypso. Still, it was Odysseus himself that Demodocus was singing about, him and Achilles, a man he never quarreled with—even if he certainly never liked him much and was not above rebuking him on occasion. Now Odysseus listened, with a smile playing around his lips, until suddenly the tears began to course down his cheeks as he remembered his companions, the exciting danger of battle, the horror of those mangled bodies, trampled underfoot by the horses, the thrill and

exhaustion at the end when Troy stood burning, and all those companions dead.

It was Alcinous who noticed the stranger's distress and quickly
called for an athletic contest, dismissing Demodocus almost midsentence. At that all the young men jumped up and proceeded to the
sporting grounds, jostling and pushing one another, stretching, exercising, while the banquet guests disposed themselves along the sides
of the area. There were many excellent young men on Scheria, and
they were all at hand, young adults, as well as boys of seventeen,
eighteen, and nineteen. Odysseus could tell from the way they were
eagerly scanning the area where the women sat that these were the
lads about whom Nausicaa had been speaking so disdainfully. They
competed, men and boys together, at running, wrestling, jumping,
discus, and boxing. When they were done, Laodamas, Alcinous' son,
surprised Odysseus by coming up to ask him if he would care to compete. It was not clear to Odysseus whether he might have been teasing, although the young man addressed him as "father stranger,"
which seemed respectful enough. Still, Odysseus answered by sug-
gesting that Laodamas was taunting him, then demurred: the hard-
ships he had endured, the sorrow he felt, and the present anxiety
over homecoming made him unfit for athletic contests.

That response inspired the haughty young aristocratic
Euryalus to observe that the stranger was unfit for athletic contests
because he was obviously of the merchant class, and their only
notion of competition was in speculation for profit. It was, of course,
true that Odysseus was shorter and stockier than the ideal of the
time, not to mention going on fifty, battle-scarred, and weather-
beaten. Once again Athena must have endowed him with special
physical beauty; otherwise, he would have presented too striking a

contrast to the young men on the playing field. Odysseus himself thought that he would have seemed too far gone even to be considered fit for competition, although Laodamas confessed to him later that he had run his eye over the stranger, estimating his chances, and immediately noticed the thighs, calves, his huge neck, noting that the stranger had quite a build, even if he did look somewhat the worse for wear.

Odysseus observed to Euryalus that men are not all the same, some are brilliant at speaking, whereas some have beautiful bodies with minds of little consequence. The annoyance he felt and could not hide led him to pick up the heaviest discus lying there and, while admitting to being in rotten shape, to throw it over the marks of all the others. His success made him cocky and he began to boast of his skill in other sports, turning it into the kind of long-winded harangue he must have heard often enough from old Nestor at Troy, until Alcinous had the good grace to interrupt.

In an ironic vein, the king said something about the Phaeaceans not being good at everything, maybe not the world's greatest athletes, but good at running. With a smile he went on to list their achievements, hoping that this fellow would tell his wife and children—obviously, he had understood the stranger's silence at the marriage proposal—how they were good at seafaring, feasting, playing the lyre, and dancing. With a chuckle, he added, and at providing clothes, hot baths, and beds. With that he clapped his hands and called out for some dancing. The boys came out to the open space and performed their dances. Then Demodocus was brought back to sing an amusing song about Aphrodite and her adulterous relationship with Ares and how her husband, Hephaestus, caught her at it; this was evidently a great favorite as the audience began to smile and laugh almost from the first line. Afterward Laodamas, the king's son, and a friend demonstrated two-man volleyball, the one throwing the ball high in the air, the other leaping up from the ground to catch it. When that was finished the two performed a dance of intricate steps while all the other young men beat out the rhythm with their feet. Odysseus spontaneously praised them to King Alcinous, who was so moved at the compliments from this wayfaring stranger that he called out to all his fellow rulers to consider giving gifts for him to bear homeward on the ship. The haughty Euryalus, who had disparaged Odysseus as a man of commerce, in turn responded to this wave of goodwill by coming forward to Odysseus and apologizing for his rudeness. As amends he offered him a beautifully worked bronze sword with a silver handle, set into a scabbard of ivory. His magnificent gesture was then repeated in the glorious gifts that all the servants of Alcinous' colleagues began to heap up before Odysseus.

Last came Alcinous holding in his arms a box of polished olive wood, set with stones on each side, an heirloom handed down from his grandfather. Inside was a bronze dagger inlaid with figures in gold and silver: a man poised to hurl a spear, his slaves before him holding shields, and in balance along the shaft of the blade a large lion outstretched, lunging at the group opposing it. The shields of the slaves were in silver, their loincloths were in gold, the hunter had a silver chiton, his spear a long line of gold, the lion massive in gold. The munificence of the Phaeaceans, the splendor of the objects, their value, the sight of them there as Arete and her helpers began to pack them away into wooden trunks brought Odysseus the deepest satisfaction. It was a kind of rehabilitation after years of desperation, deprivation, and danger. The gifts, the men and women surrounding him in whom he sensed such goodwill, his feeling then of surrender, the momentary shedding of his habitual anxiety and paranoia, all made it a moment that Odysseus never forgot. He knew he was returning home a richer man than when he had left Troy, his ship filled with plunder.

Another banquet was laid on for the evening by Alcinous, who was clearly thrilled at this exciting interruption of their otherwise placid lives on Scheria. As was the custom of the time, the leading figure, the most kingly, received from the populace vast quantities of food—grain, wine, meat—and it was his social obligation to fete the community on a regular basis. In this way, through the frequent sacrifice of animals for the meat at the banquets, the community gave thanks, offered prayers to the gods, and kept their place holy. Communal growing and harvesting, communal preparation of the meals, climaxing in communal eating developed social cohesion in the Bronze Age; this survived, if only as a faint echo of behavior and attitude, into the later centuries of ancient Greek culture. In its way it was a grand-scale version—with far more serious implications—of what our contemporaries try to achieve at something like a church supper, to which everyone brings a home-cooked offering.

As a preparation for the night's festivities, the men and boys of the island stripped and immersed themselves in pools of hot sulfurous water, which were filled from a steaming spring coming from a cleft in a craggy slope. Then Odysseus returned to the guest quarters, where the maids bathed him in a large copper tub filled with perfumed water, rubbed him down with perfumed oil, and dressed him in a new tunic with matching mantle. As he was entering the banquet hall, Nausicaa stopped him at the door to have a private moment with him, to say good-bye, reminding him that he owed his life to her first, above all the people of Scheria. Her appearance and the emotion of her speech filled Odysseus with the strongest urge ever to remain on Scheria, to start life anew. He glanced at her long, elegant neck, at the tight rosy, dusky skin, so smooth, in its descent into her décolletage. By reflex he stretched out his hand to study the contrast of its roughness, the wrinkles and veins of his wrist proclaiming the degradation that age and living had inflicted upon it. It was time to go home. Nonetheless, her few quiet sentences reminded him so clearly of the transaction on the beach that he was prompted to go beyond the pretty words of farewell the occasion called for. Looking her in the face, he promised to pray to her as though she were a goddess all the days of his life, recalling them both to that moment on the beach when he had likened her to Artemis and thought to offer her prayers—that moment fresh, pregnant with possibilities for the two of them.

When Demodocus was led in again for the evening's entertainment, Odysseus signaled to a servant to present him with the choicest piece of meat as a gesture of his respect for the blind old singer. After they had eaten, Odysseus complimented Demodocus on how true to the events of the Trojan War his songs were, then asked him to sing of the episode when the Achaeans hid themselves in the great wooden horse. It is always a treat to hear a narrative in which one figures as an important element and Odysseus was enjoying the song Demodocus sang, until once again he could not control the grief that shook him, nor the tears that streamed down his cheeks.

No more could King Alcinous control himself at this sight. The curiosity that had been building since the day before, the speculation at night he and Arete had been tossing back and forth between them, now began to spill over as he glanced across the room to see Arete looking fixedly right at him from where she sat with Nausicaa and the other women. Alcinous recognized the command in her gaze and again he stopped Demodocus in midsentence. After politely sympathizing with the stranger's deep emotions suddenly on display, he asked Odysseus to tell his name, his country, his parents. He wanted to know why the stranger had burst into tears when he heard songs of Troy and the Achaeans, venturing the observation that the gods brought these disasters upon mankind so that later generations could weave them into their traditional narratives.

There was dead silence in the room. Even the serving people stayed their task of collecting plates and utensils to hear the answer. Curiosity had ruled everyone on the island of Scheria all day. Odysseus leaned forward in his chair, congratulating Alcinous on the magnificence of the banquet at which they were gathered, praising the singer who had brought him to tears, remarking that food, drink, and well-sung tales are the natural components of a brilliant evening. With that he paused, then spoke his name, called out the name Laertes, his father; Ithaca, his island home; Neritos, the landmark mountain peak on Ithaca, then the names of all the islands adjacent. He avowed that no place was sweeter than his homeland, that try as they might neither Calypso nor Circe could persuade him to stay with them. Nothing is sweeter, he repeated, than parents and country. With that as his prelude, he began the recitation of the tumultous years of his homecoming. Evenings spent narrating these events to Calypso had given him a repertory of words, phrases, story lines, all in the style of the traditional singer. So he was fluent that evening as he held the court of Alcinous and Arete spellbound for hours.

He had in mind to give them a sampling of those ten years, going on until he sensed that his audience was weary. After several hours, when he was somewhere in his description of the voyage to the Underworld, he felt a great weariness come over him. After he had told of speaking with Tiresias and with his mother, Anticleia, he felt that it was time to stop, so he introduced a stock piece, the catalogue of famous women, something singers can toss in at will as filler, a bridge, or here—what he hoped—an obvious conclusion. And indeed, when he paused, there was a deep silence in the room until Arete spoke up to sing Odysseus' praises and to claim him as her very own guest who deserved even more gifts. Echeneos, who, Odysseus noticed, had been the one to remind Alcinous of his royal position, quickly broke in to praise Arete's sentiments, then reminded the assembled group that Alcinous was the one to make the royal decisions concerning the guest.

It was just like the time Echeneos told Alcinous to move the suppliant out of the hearth and into a chair. Alcinous started, as though still entranced by Odysseus' narrative, and in a booming voice promised new gifts in abundance. Odysseus, who was such an adept at irony, dealing it and noting it, was puzzled when Alcinous began to praise him for his skill at storytelling, noting that the world was full of mountebanks, liars, and thieves who went about telling falsehoods, whereas Odysseus, with all the technique of a professional, was obviously telling the true story of his war years and beyond. Then Alcinous forcefully asked Odysseus to tell more about the Underworld, wanting to know if, for instance, he had met any of his former fellow officers in the Achaean army at Troy. The night is young, he kept insisting, and the story fascinating. Odysseus felt he had no choice but to continue. It was finally the middle of the night as he reached the moment when he washed up on Calypso's island, at which point he was about to repeat himself and so he stopped.

Again they sat in silence until Alcinous urged each of his fellow guests to give Odysseus major objects of precious metals as further evidence of their great friendship. With that they separated for bed, each to his own house. On the following day, another round of feasting ensued with more singing by Demodocus, all of which Odysseus was forced to endure patiently, smiling affably, while in his heart he was raging to get going. At last the sun set, and the entire town went down to the harbor where the ship stood. His gifts were stowed away on board, he settled down on soft bedding, and the crew bent forward to their oars, and off they went. Odysseus was able to recount nothing of the voyage back to Ithaca because he fell into a deep sleep. When he thought about it, he wondered if possibly he had been drugged; perhaps the Phaeaceans wanted to spare him the discomfort of a long trip. The next thing he knew he was waking up on a sandy beach, still lying atop his soft bedding with the coverlet pulled up over him.

CHAPTER 5

• ◆ •

KING

Wʜᴇɴ ᴛʜᴇ Pʜᴀᴇᴀᴄᴇᴀɴs deposited the sleeping Odysseus on the beach at Ithaca, he awoke to a very different country from the one he had left twenty years earlier to join Agamemnon's expedition to Troy. The political structure in Ithaca was now unstable. Laertes, the king, had retired from the city. As the young men of the area began to congregate at his palace, somehow Laertes could not cope with the influx, the energy, the naked hunger for power, and the ambition of these men. His wife, Anticleia, had died: everyone said it was of a broken heart, she missed her son Odysseus so. The death changed Laertes. Some said he had become simpleminded, the way some old people seem to fall off, no longer able to control their lives. He had set himself up in a modest peasant house on land he owned in the hills, sleeping on the ground, just as the peasant slaves did, dressed in rags, waking each day to work in the orchards and fields as much as he could. Penelope sent an old Sicilian woman to cook for him, get him to change his clothes at least once in a while, and wash them. Now in his old age Laertes was doing what he loved best, pruning, tying up, and spading in new plants.

Most of the men of Odysseus' generation, leaders of the various islands and the mainland territory under Laertes' rule, had died at Troy or been lost at sea on the voyage home. The vacuum of leadership was not about to be filled by Telemachus, so unsure of himself and untested, who at that moment was not even on the island. Weeks before he had gone off to the mainland in search of his father—if not in reality then psychologically. Odysseus was the only male in his generation of the royal family. It had been the same for his father, Laertes, and for Arkeisios before Laertes; there were no collateral relatives. Telemachus seemed too young to be in the running. The crown was up for grabs, or, rather what seemed to be the case, in the power of the queen, if she were indeed widowed, to bestow on whatever man she chose, just as the widowed Queen Jocasta's marriage to Oedipus at Thebes made him king. The prospect of Penelope's possible remarriage kept a gang of men camping out in the palace for years, hoping to get the nod from Penelope when she finally gave in and accepted as fact that Odysseus was dead and she should remarry.

The ancient idea of hospitality, which required that the host, in this case, nominally the absent Odysseus, offer food and drink to any visitor, put a significant burden on his household. On the surface of things if a suitor stopped by to present himself to Penelope as a reasonable candidate for marriage, she or her son or Mentor, the old family adviser whom Odysseus had left in charge, would ask him to dinner and to spend the night. The problem in this case was that men had begun to arrive in droves, and they expected to sleep over if they came from any kind of distance. Furthermore, they obstinately refused to take seriously Penelope's often expressed disinclination to consider their petitions, preferring to wait near at hand until a trustworthy messenger arrived with the news of her husband's death. While they waited, they consumed vast—epic, one might say—amounts of meat and drink, which resulted in drastic depletion of royal land and herds. Many of them, of course, were residents of the immediate vicinity; many more while staying in the area began to consider themselves locals.

The guest-host obligation collided with the royal banqueting obligation, which imposed upon the local regal figure the necessity to maintain a nightly table for the presentation of food to the community. (Melanthius, the goatherd, we note, felt comfortable sitting down at these communal tables; it must have been open to every male.) Of course, it may well have been that bankrupting the royal family was a deliberate strategy of the suitors. These resources had already significantly suffered from the absence of Odysseus and the tentative behavior of his son; there appears to have been no decent management, although Telemachus, by at least nominally hosting the evening banquet and managing the family farmland, kept himself in position as heir apparent. He seems to have had little power. When he wanted to sail to the mainland, he had to borrow a ship from a friendly man of the town named Noemon. Mentor seemed to have no authority either, since when Telemachus had not returned and Noemon wanted his ship back, he went to the chief suitors about the matter rather than approaching the palace manager.

The young men who crowded Odysseus' palace were considerably younger than Penelope, unmarried men who sought a chance at the kingship even if it meant taking on a wife demonstrably older. Most prominent families had sent their eldest son to fight with Odysseus at Troy; second sons would have taken over the management of the family estates, leaving the youngest to plan another way of establishing himself. In Christian Europe provision for such sons was easier. In addition to the land and the army, European gentry had the church and the university for their sons, for whom no comparable sinecures existed in Odysseus' time. What better means of advancement than inheriting lands and a throne by marrying a widowed queen! In the previous three or four years, since Laertes had taken to the hills, these fellows had created havoc in the palace. Young men in groups, especially arrogant young men, born to exercise their bodies and learn to defend themselves, when sitting about all evening drinking, tend to drink too much, to force themselves on the serving staff, to get into fights, to piss and vomit where they shouldn't, in general to make life miserable for everyone else in the place. Here there was no one to restrain them, certainly not Mentor, and not young Telemachus, either. Other than Laertes, Telemachus had had no male role model, specifically no one born to authority. The suitors who saw him as a potential threat to their plans shunned him when they could; he despised them. It was all very well for Telemachus to seek the company of Eumaeus, to pass time listening to the swineherd reminisce about the extraordinary virtues of his father and the happy days gone by, but that was another kind of education altogether. Very recently, when Telemachus had tried to remonstrate with the suitors in an assembly that he had called to discuss his situation, he so lost his cool that he burst into tears and threw the scepter on the floor. Kings are not made of such stuff as that, an observation made by everyone who witnessed his performance or heard of it later.

That unhappy scene took place over a month before Odysseus landed on Ithaca. Since that unfortunate moment, Telemachus had set out for the mainland to get what information he could about his long absent father, but what he acquired instead was his first real adult friend, Peisistratus. It is amazing what a new friend can do; Telemachus seemed to have turned some kind of corner, a dramatic change for the better. Peisistratus was the son born late in life to Nestor, king of Pylos, Odysseus' colleague in arms at Troy. Old Nestor, in that ironic twist so frequent in human history, having come through the war that claimed his son Antilochus, not to mention so many other brave and noble young men, survived the voyage home to take his place once more on the throne at possibly seventy if not eighty years of age.

Peisistratus, whom Telemachus met in Pylos, was a constant revelation in deportment and attitude for the inexperienced boy. They went together to visit Menelaus and Helen at Sparta, where, as was the custom of the time, they shared a bed. The monthlong intimacy changed Telemachus forever. One might say that the two men were made for each other, which does not mean that they had a sexual relationship—even as it allows for the possibility of one, either real or fantasized in a culture where males were not compromised by eroticizing other males. His lonely childhood left Telemachus preternaturally insecure as he approached adulthood. He seemed not to have had facial hair when he set out for the mainland, which it was remarked he started to sprout soon after his return from Sparta. It is perhaps nonsense to claim that in this brief time Telemachus, as they say, grew up. Nonetheless, as later events would show, he was now what one would expect of his father's son, a staunch ally in the fight against the suitors.

Telemachus estimated the number of suitors to be 108, plus eight servants; beyond that he was not sure of the loyalty of Medon, the herald, or Phemius, the court singer. Twelve suitors were from Ithaca proper, and were, as he pointed out when he recalled these names for his father, considered to be the very best men of the island.

This seems to be an index of the waning popularity of the royal household, indicative of the immense task confronting Odysseus if he wanted to win back the position he had once held in the community.

Odysseus was soon to get to know the suitors firsthand when he went among them disguised as a beggar. Among these men, three were significant for the force of their characters: Eurymachus, Antinous, and Amphinomus. Telemachus himself once remarked that Eurymachus was the best man on the island, noting that the people of Ithaca respected him "as though he were a god." On another occasion, he cited Eurymachus' approval when he himself, as presumptive lord of the manor, was granting a request, throwing into relief the ambiguous power relationships in the palace. It seems open to question how much popular support Odysseus had retained among the people during his twenty-year absence. When Mentor, in the presence of the suitors, rebuked the people of the island for not coming to the aid of their royal family, for having forgotten how like a father to his people Odysseus was, he certainly lends support for the negative view. Eurymachus, in that sense, must have posed a real political challenge to the returning Odysseus.

Eurymachus may have conned the locals, but closer familiarity with him reveals a duplicitous nature. He could be extravagant in praising Penelope, declaring that if all Achaean men knew how ravishingly beautiful she was, there would be nonstop traffic to her front door, even as all the while he was sleeping with the slave girl Melantho, whom Penelope had raised as a kind of surrogate daughter. Of course, offering verbal bouquets to one lady while enjoying sex with another is not all that unusual, but in this instance it is part of a pattern. He could also assure Penelope that he would let no one harm Telemachus because of his own treasured memory of

Odysseus holding him as a boy in his lap, feeding him choice bits from the table, while at the same time he was plotting her son's murder.

Eurymachus was mean-spirited and cowardly as well. When later on he taunted a beggar (Odysseus in disguise) about asking for money rather than getting an honest job, and heard in response a spirited challenge to a contest in plowing and soldiering, he became so infuriated, not to mention defensive, that he picked up a footstool and hurled it at the so-called beggar. Such was his mean nature; perhaps it is telling that the malicious goatherd Melanthius loved him. Some time later (on the day of reckoning, so to speak), when the beggar revealed himself to be Odysseus, come to avenge the mistreatment of his goods and family, Eurymachus immediately put the blame for everything on Antinous who, having just been killed, could not argue the falsehood of the assertion.

If Eurymachus was a nasty piece of work, Antinous was thoroughly vicious. Telemachus is known to have declared that Antinous compulsively worked to make other people angry, and Penelope, when remarking how much she loathed all the suitors, singled out Antinous, calling him a "black death." A coldly analytical man, Antinous was typically enraged at first when he discovered that Telemachus had escaped surveillance and gone off to the mainland, but then in a cold fury realized that the suitors would have a perfect opportunity to get rid of him upon his return. He arranged for a ship to lie off the coast to ambush him. Telemachus eluded the trap by putting in at another part of the island, whereupon Antinous argued that they would have to kill him anywhere they found him ("on the road, wherever"), so that he would not lay the details of the ambush before the people ("the people are no longer so much on our side").

In a matter-of-fact way, he foresaw dividing the dead Telemachus' lands and possessions while granting his mother possession of the palace.

Perhaps Antinous' insecurities stemmed from childhood. His father, as Penelope reminded him once in public, came as a fugitive to Ithaca and it was Odysseus who had protected him. She had added this last detail because Antinous had just snarled at Eumaeus, the swineherd, for introducing the beggar into the palace : "What do we need another beggar for? They eat up all your master's food." He is on record as speaking viciously to all those who could not fight back, going so far as to threaten another beggar with deportation, enslavement, and physical disfigurement. When two of Odysseus' loyal servants burst into tears seeing their master's bow brought out, Antinous derided the honest emotion the two men displayed by coldly giving the Bronze Age equivalent of "get a grip!" His fundamental insecurity revealed itself again in the smarmy way he chose to placate Telemachus after the young man's tears in the assembly. He forced a smile, took Telemachus by hand, urged him to come along with him to dinner, and promised to get him what he wanted—in short, he was entirely civil but in a phony way.

Only Amphinomus, the man from Doulichion, another part of the domain, seems to have stood out for the civility of his behavior. Certainly Penelope was known to prefer him for what he had to say, pointing out that it showed a "good mind." He seemed to have been blessed with a sanguine personality; everyone remarked on his being able to laugh when the other suitors were seething at the fact that Telemachus had managed to evade his would-be killers waiting in ambush. He could be moral as well, even if not consistently so, answering Antinous' insistence that Telemachus must be summarily murdered when the ambush had failed by saying that he would have no part in the killing of someone of royal blood without the direct and clear assent of Zeus. Later, when an eagle flew overhead with a pigeon in its beak, he took this as an omen of failure for the suitors' plan to murder Telemachus, and urged them good-naturedly to plan banqueting instead. How ironic then, when Odysseus had revealed himself and begun his battle against the suitors, that it was Telemachus who stabbed Amphinomus through the back between his shoulder blades as the man made ready to spring at Odysseus with his sword. Most observers have said that it was a further irony that Amphinomus seemed to have lost heart with the suitors' aggressive tactics by then. His demeanor in response to the cruelty perpetrated against the two beggars would argue for this. Indeed, when Eurymachus threw a footstool at the disguised Odysseus, it was against Amphinomus' knee that this beggar crouched, and Amphinomus was the man who moments later spoke out to urge an end to the anger and the violence, to remind the suitors that their targets were in the house of Odysseus, and thus protected, even if the lord of the manor were absent or dead. But Amphinomus stayed in the game until the end; in his disguise Odysseus had tried to warn this seemingly nice man, but Amphinomus was too far gone in complicity, as is clear from his waffling over the fate of Telemachus.

The behavior of Penelope is a complicating factor in analyzing the situation. As the suitors sometimes complained, she herself was capable of deceit, or at least was not above misleading them. They grumbled, for instance, that she sent them oral messages via the slave women, individually encouraging this one or that. It seems from this vantage point to be an obvious, wise stratagem of divide and conquer, in the sense that she did not want them to think of themselves as having a common interest or goal but rather to remain forever individual competitors for her hand. Her delaying tactic with the weaving of the shroud for Laertes is famous—that is, announcing that she would choose a consort when the shroud was finished, weaving it by day, unraveling it each night for some three years, until one of the maids more loyal to the suitors than to her revealed the secret. If they had not spent nights drinking and dancing, and days no doubt nursing hangovers, the suitors might have noticed themselves that Penelope was taking an inordinately long time at her weaving. At the time of Odysseus' return it had been a year since the discovery so she was under that added pressure to choose a successor to her husband.

Penelope is one of the greater mysteries for any student of Odysseus' life. What did she really want? While her two cousins share an interesting history of sexual abandon, Penelope will always be remembered for her enduring chastity in the face of so much constant pressure over the years from a household full of lusty young males who wanted to bed her. Her cousin Clytemnestra started sleeping with Agamemnon's cousin once her husband had gone off to Troy (even if one could argue that, rather than for her personal validation or recreation, the sex act had become an act of revenge for the woman who had witnessed her husband sacrifice their daughter for his career ambitions). Penelope was not, however, some pallid, perfect opposite of her errant cousins. It is perfectly possible to see erotic games being played when the suitors complain that she led them on by sending them messages of hope via her slaves. Not only that but one night, as she told it, she dreamt that an eagle swooped down and killed her twenty pet geese, which she had fed and housed for so long. She was reduced to tears, suffering the loss of her pet geese, even though the eagle assumed the voice of a human to tell her that just as he, the eagle, has killed the geese so would her husband return to kill the suitors. Penelope may not have wanted to go to bed with these importunate louts, but it is always sexually stimulating to flirt and be surrounded by so much male animal energy. It must have been a kick to dress up, as she is said to have done, cover the lower part of her face with a diaphanous veil, and descend the staircase into the main hall where the suitors were gathered, watch them react, and see them get weak in the knees, then race off home to get still more and better gifts so as to woo her successfully.

The very terms by which she would remarry were conflicting, changing, and ambiguous. There was one idea that she would return to the home of Icarius, her father, and that those who sought her hand in marriage would pay court there, give gifts, receive them, and generally behave in the fashion to which males in the Bronze Age were acculturated. This tactic would favor Telemachus, since Penelope would leave the throne at Ithaca behind for her son to occupy with a bride of his own at his side. Nonetheless, Telemachus, curiously enough, objected at one point, arguing that the family did not have the resources to repay Icarius the bride price Odysseus had given for Penelope. (It seems doubtful that Odysseus had paid a bride price considering that she was his reward for counseling Tyndareus on strategy for quelling the competition among Helen's suitors.) Telemachus may have simply been playing for time, thinking to delay things until he felt ready to marry. It is always difficult to get at Telemachus' ambitions; at one point he had said publicly that the monarchy did not interest him, so long as his estates and palace were intact. Certainly one has to attribute Penelope's famous fidelity, her playing the twenty-year-long waiting game, to a mother's determination to stick things out until her son was comfortably on the throne. But more than a mother, she was a dynast, faithful to the principle of monarchy that was embodied in her husband's family on the island of Ithaca. Romantics entirely misunderstand Penelope.

An alternative maneuver was for Penelope to choose among the suitors present in the house. This is what most of them preferred, and Antinous famously said something like "take our gifts, and don't argue, but whatever you do, we are not leaving this site until you choose another husband." This scenario would seem to have doomed Telemachus, because the new husband would hardly have endured the kind of competition an adult son alive and well on the island would offer, especially when Penelope was probably too old to bear the second husband any heirs. The advantage was to the suitors who wanted more than anything else to be king. Penelope was not above playing one idea off against the other, obviously hoping against hope that her husband would return, as they say in melodramas and folk tales, in the nick of time.

When Odysseus awoke on the beach at Ithaca, he recognized nothing. The shock easily aroused the paranoia that his experiences had fostered in him, even after he had counted the Phaeaceans' many gifts and found nothing missing; he was likewise plunged into a depression that only betrayal can produce. As he was to learn moments later, Athena had made the familiar landscape unrecognizable. She never offered a motive for doing so, but it is not hard to imagine that she wished to instill in her protégé at the outset a strenuous resistance to accepting things for what they might seem to be.

That moment on the beach is certainly the single most important in this man's complicated life. As he surveyed with dismay the unfamiliar surroundings, there appeared before him a young man, a shepherd as he remembered it, a young and delicate boy. Odysseus recalled thinking—when he took a look at the facial structure, skin tones, and body build—that he seemed more like the child of kings than the son of rustic peasants. He fell to his knees supplicating the lad, begging to know where he was. The shepherd boy proceeded to list the well-known geographical landmarks of Odysseus' native land, ending his recital with words to the effect that this, sir, is Ithaca. Athena then lifted the mist, or whatever it was that had addled his wits, and there before him was his familiar Ithaca. He remembered the shock, and how in an effort to keep control he opened his mouth and told a lie.

Falsehood, of which he was so often accused at Troy and thereafter, was probably his best developed mode of defense. He himself did not, of course, ever say this in so many words. To his biographer, however, it seems clear enough. Lying is an exceptional device for anyone who wishes to control all situations and manipulate others. It enables one to mask a display of honest emotion, which is dangerous because it exposes vulnerability. Odysseus had hoped to land on Ithaca and knowingly creep up on friend and foe alike. His initial ignorance of the landscape threw him off balance, the sudden revelation that it was indeed Ithaca more so. He did not know by whom, but he knew that he was being manipulated. Rather than surrender to the honest emotion that such a cascade of surprises can produce, which might well have rendered him vulnerable to the shepherd boy's gaze, he chose instead to give a false identity. Thus, as Odysseus no doubt imagined it, he would have the instant high ground of knowing something of which everyone else was ignorant (i.e., that what he was saying was untrue), the ultimate reassurance in dicey situations.

But, of course, he was not aware that the winsome shepherd lad was actually Athena in disguise, who knew everything in the heart and mind of Odysseus. He claimed to be a fugitive from Crete, where he had murdered the son of Idomeneus, who tried to deprive him of his share of plunder taken from Troy, and a lot of other details, making his falsehood more a fictional narrative moving in the direction of a novella than a simple lie. The extensive details allowed him momentarily to assume the character of his creation, doing what inveterate liars know is essential: creating enough details to make an entire world, which will have the same substance as the real one. This is always the mark, for example, of successful adulterers.

Athena's reaction to this behavior was indeed the high point of Odysseus' life, his validation, a triumph of reassurance, support, and love rarely vouchsafed to human beings in the whole of recorded history. The goddess suddenly dropped her disguise and appeared instead as a larger-than-life human figure, a beautiful, sparkling woman. Athena had left off her characteristic armor, her aegis, choosing to present herself in her other cult guise, a woman skilled in handicrafts, obvious to the eye by the way her experienced, long, dextrous fingers ran affectionately and appraisingly over the needlework of the seams of her gown, proudly, as only one who has made them would be able to do.

She smiled and stroked his hand, saying something that he, in his surprise and excitement, somehow remembered as: "Odysseus, such a con man, always looking for the deal, ready to grab whatever you can get your hands on, who could ever beat you in trickery, even when your opponent is a god? You sly puss, so crafty when you're being inconsistent, you just won't let go, here you are in your native land, and you keep right on lying and cheating, it is your very nature, you, the best of mortals when it comes to planning and to speaking, and just like me, the goddess known for her strategies and successes."

Odysseus tried to make a little defense of his immediate instinct for falsehood, to rationalize his suspicion and mistrust on the basis of the many disasters that he had recently suffered. He ended his remarks true to form, going on the offensive, claiming that the goddess might well be teasing him, and that what she assured him was Ithaca was in fact some other place. Athena, broadly smiling, would have none of his protestations. It was why she could never desert him, she claimed, because he was so clever, so rational, so coolheaded—he never missed a trick.

She also apologized to him for her lack of support during all the perils that had beset him in his travels; this had been out of respect for her uncle Poseidon, she claimed, whose enmity Odysseus had earned by his blinding of the Cyclops. She might have gone on to say what a stunningly uncharacteristic act his self-indulgent mocking of the Cyclops had been, as every student of Odysseus' life always avers.

When Athena repeated to Odysseus what his mother had told him in the Underworld about the palace and his wife besieged by suitors, he and the goddess plotted how to overthrow them. On the surface of things, one might imagine that the returning Odysseus, beloved king of his lands, could have walked through one village lane after another, gathering the peasants around him in a display of feudal loyalty, until, massed outside the palace shouting and threatening its inmates, he and they would have effected the suitors' capitulation. Or, after a bit of time, starved them out. Apparently this was not an option, not even discussed, which speaks eloquently to the fragility of his power base on Ithaca. The plan to which the two agreed was that she would transform him so that his skin and hair and costume would suggest a homeless wandering beggar. Under cover of this disguise, he would then make his way into the palace, where he could somehow wreak destruction on the suitors. Odysseus decided that assuming the appearance of a person from the lowest ranks of society would give him the opportunity to test the loyalty of the servants, who would have to be his most significant allies. Athena quickly reminded him of Telemachus, whom she said she would motivate to return home as soon as she could make her way to Sparta and into his dream world. She confessed that she had made herself into a dream as a similar stratagem to get Nausicaa down to the beach, washing clothes, so that she could come across the newly awakened Odysseus.

It was important for Odysseus to enter the palace and penetrate the society of the suitors in order to legitimate the murder of these men in the eyes of the community. He had every intention of killing the suitors, but to do this openly required appropriate motives. If he, in disguise as the beggar, could provoke the suitors to maltreat him, then he could claim some kind of lèse-majesté. Beggar or no, he would still be Odysseus, son of Laertes, etc.; the body maltreated would be that of a king. More to the point, perhaps, he had in mind the sacred code of hospitality, invested with all the awe and power of Zeus, god of hospitality. He had been its beneficiary time and again in the past twenty years; he knew that the people of Ithaca and the adjacent lands piously subscribed to the code. If—as a suppliant, a stranger, even if a dirty, ugly, old beggar—he were abused, this in his mind would constitute reason to exact the most awful punishment upon the suitors.

The Phaeaceans had left Odysseus at the very opposite end of the island from the royal palace, not far in fact from the outlying pig farm managed by Eumaeus, his childhood friend. It was into this dwelling that he stumbled in his new character as a travel-weary homeless beggar. Eumaeus received him kindly, something Odysseus was never to forget. The house, like almost all habitations of the time, had dirt floors. Its ceilings and walls were blackened by the smoke from the open hearth, where fire was the only source of interior illumination. The swineherd went to the stone-enclosed pigsty, chose an especially good animal, and slaughtered and butchered it, setting out the choicest portions of meat for the stranger's dinner. As they ate, Eumaeus (who obviously did not often have visitors) was profuse in his declaration of loyalty to the family of Odysseus, harsh in his condemnation of the suitors, and shrewd in his assessment of the heavy toll their evening entertainments were exacting on the resources of the royal household.

Eumaeus told the beggar that he intended in the next day or two to take him to the royal palace because the swineherd did not have the means to support another person in his forlorn little hut. But before they managed to set off for the palace, Telemachus put in an appearance. He had returned from his visit to the mainland and come straight off the ship. He had taken it into his head, as he explained to Eumaeus, to order his crew to set him down at the far end of the island so that he could visit the farms and estimate the progress of the harvest, ordering them to continue on into the harbor of the town behind which the palace rose on a hill. When later on he and his father discovered that he had inadvertently escaped the suitors' ship, which lay in ambush nearer to the town harbor, they ascribed his impulse to land at the far end of the island not to lucky chance but to the agency of Athena. As Odysseus was to say long afterward in describing this period, he was never in the slightest doubt about the ultimate success of what seemed like a dubious enterprise, considering the numbers of suitors, because he knew that he had Athena at his side. One would be hard put to find divine love and concern of this intensity expressed by any other deity for any other mortal. Athena's love for Odysseus was unique, and in that relentless and cruel symmetry of the ancient world equaled in intensity and perseverance only by Hera's hatred of Heracles.

Eumaeus left to tell Penelope that her son was safe, apologizing to the beggar for leaving him behind. As the swineherd explained, he wanted to get the news to her in a hurry, as well as to see what the suitors were up to now that their quarry had escaped their ambush. While he was gone, the old beggar, suddenly transformed into an identifiable, but older version of the high-hearted handsome young husband and father who had set out for Troy twenty years earlier, announced to the startled Telemachus that he was Odysseus, his father. Athena, they had to assume, was the agency for the transformation. It was a miracle. Telemachus believed in miracles—he had been waiting for this one all his life, as he told his mother later. The two clasped each other almost to the point of pain, so strong was the need to feel the other close, crying with deep groans. The tears that the two of them shed were a lamentation of the years of their separation, when Odysseus never knew his son and the young man never knew his father. It was a loss for which there is no reparation, and so they cried.

As they sat together, Odysseus told his son about the war years, about his adventures wandering the Mediterranean. Telemachus, for his part, told his father of his travels to Pylos, how shy he had been, how insecure in his table manners and other social graces when he met old Nestor and the rest of his court, watching with awe as Nestor performed the religious rites in a series of festivals, feeling ashamed at the squalor and chaos he had left behind at the palace in Ithaca. He described to his father—with a flush of joy at the memory—meeting Peisistratus, how this bright, serious son of Nestor had taken him in hand, and off they had gone to visit Helen and Menelaus at Sparta. Telemachus claimed all his life that he could not have pulled off that visit without his friend, Peisistratus; he was such a country rube, and even though going on for twenty-two, acted like a boy of sixteen—that's how naïve he was. The palace of Menelaus was the very height of elegance and grandeur, the service and its management perfection. That, at least, was what Peisistratus whispered in his ear from the moment they walked across the grand portal.

He told his father that when Helen made her entrance into the throne room, he felt the hush—more than a sound, the very air was stilled—that her beauty inspired in the courtiers and guests. She walked directly toward him first—it made him tremble—and looked at him hard; in his confusion he somehow heard her voice, identifying him as the son of Odysseus. No one else seemed to have noticed, certainly not Menelaus, who looked perpetually hypnotized in the presence of his dazzling spouse. Helen and Menelaus took the young men into their confidence, sometimes in the evenings when perhaps everyone had drunk more wine than they should, telling them stories of the days at Troy (of course, the two of them from very different perspectives). Telemachus often flinched when the malice became pronounced, looking over to Peisistratus to gauge how to react; it was his only experience of a royal marriage. Later, when Peisistratus and Telemachus had bid the king and queen good night, he said that the two men lay in bed together in their fragrant, breeze-filled portico and laughed, recalling the royal couple. There is nothing like shared contempt to cement a bond.

Telemachus told his father the friendship with Peisistratus was something he imagined that he would never know again. Odysseus, whenever he thought about it, had to admit he had never really had a friend. He remembered going to visit his grandfather with Eurylochus, but that boy had been imposed upon him, because young men went traveling in twosomes. His parents arranged for Eurylochus because he was the younger brother of Ctimene's husband; it was an effort to endure him then, he remembered that very clearly; worse still when they were at Troy together; but worst of all on the long voyage home. Odysseus had even admitted publicly that he was not that sorry when Eurylochus had drowned at sea; after all, he had disobeyed specific orders. As Telemachus talked on, Odysseus thought of Achilles and Patroclus, Diomedes and Sthenelus, the two Ajaxes always together, Idomeneus and Meriones, he could go on and on, he supposed, but had to admit, did indeed admit, that he had never really had a special friend, a buddy, a companion.

Revealing himself to Telemachus had been a crucial step forward in Odysseus' grand plan, but there was much, much more to be done. How Odysseus finally overcame the suitors and regained his throne is an event famously told in many narratives. It owed much, of course, to Athena's help, especially in the last crucial moments of the battle. In the beginning, however, Odysseus depended upon his beggarly disguise to enable him to determine friend and foe. When the suitors physically abused him, he made mental note of it. When certain household help were particularly malicious, such as Melanthius the goatherd and the maidservant Melantho, he did not forget.

Athena quickly transformed Odysseus back into a beggar before Eumaeus returned from his mission; it was not time yet to tell the loyal swineherd. Telemachus had gone ahead to the palace, and then on the next day, as he had promised, Eumaeus accompanied the disguised Odysseus. At the gate of the paved road that led up toward the palace Telemachus was talking with some suitors who had just arrived. He was there, as he explained later, in his anxiety that everything should proceed perfectly as his father entered this dangerous space. He looked about to ensure that all was in order and his eye fell on a pile of trash and dung where lay the pitiful half-dead body of his childhood pet and companion, the dog Swifty, twenty years old now. To his horror and consternation, Swifty, having weakly lifted his head at the sound of the voice of Odysseus, began to wag his tail, and with the greatest effort pathetically raised himself onto his front legs, and then, wheezing in a raucous way, onto his rear legs. Out of the corner of his eye, Telemachus saw his father give the dog a quick glance. Just as Telemachus thought he might have to run some kind of interference, the dog, who had laboriously clambered down from his wretched resting place, pitched forward, chin skidding the ground, and fell mercifully dead.

The palace appeared as Odysseus remembered it. A narrow stone tower to the left of the gate reminded newcomers that this was a military fortification as much as a residence. The high entrance gate formed by two immense stone piers had been freshly painted, it seemed to him: the yellow and red trim, scrolls, and rosettes gleamed forth in the morning sun. The paving underfoot had been stuccoed, then painted with black octopuses, their thin wavy legs cutting diagonally in a formal pattern from side to side. Eumaeus and Odysseus entered under the gate, passing between two columns with capitals carved with flowers and fruits and painted in pink and green. The vestibule was decorated with frescoes on each wall, depicting long processionals. On the one side, rows of horses dominated, their massed legs forming a kind of band beneath the line of the brightly ornamented and painted carriages, in which stood tall women in profile with flowing hair and baskets of ritual instruments. On the other side, tall males in profile, soldiers with shields and spears marched in a line, two by two. Painted over the door to the throne room were two pink griffins facing each other.

The large room used for banqueting where the suitors tended to congregate was off to the side; like the throne room, it measured some fifty feet by thirty feet, its enormous roof supported by two rows of stout stone columns. It was darker in this area because farther from the source of natural light, although the fire in the hearth did give off some illumination, its flames reflected in the weaponry and shields that hung in neat rows on the two short walls of the room. On the long walls, paintings of gardens and fields, behind which was a blue river, suggested light psychologically even if not producing it in reality. High on the walls were the familar rows of painted birds in flight, soaring over the gardens, fields, and stream underneath. The floor below had a design of blue scallops and red spirals painted on the stuccoed area around the edge of the room; the surface of the main floor of the banquet room was packed dirt.

The suitors there that day were variously engaged. Some were deep in concentration over a game not unlike checkers, in which polished stones were moved around on a board with painted lines. Others were playing at marbles, a game they had invented, in which a relatively large marble they called "the queen" was the target and whoever hit a smaller marble off the queen, and succeeded in doing so a second time in succession was considered to be destiny's serious candidate for the hand of Queen Penelope. Still others stood in a group taking turns performing as jugglers—a skill they were in the process of learning from a traveling team of acrobats, who themselves stood in the courtyard balancing one on top of the other in the hope of being given a free meal, a bed, and perhaps a gift.

The suitors, true to form, were vicious in their treatment of the vagabond, insinuating that he could easily work and not beg if he chose to, a commonplace response from century to century and culture to culture of people who do little or nothing themselves and live entirely on the labor of others. They rebuked Eumaeus for bringing another mouth to feed into the palace, insolently dismissing the sacred claims of the wayfarer, ignoring as well their own monstrous depredations of the palace larder—both of which Eumaeus did not hesitate to throw right back at them, his usually quiet voice deepening with harshness and anger. This seemed to provoke Antinous, who showed his hostility by throwing a stool at Odysseus in his beggar's clothing. Odysseus remembered a certain kind of grim pleasure that possessed him in contemplating the way these men so relentlessly courted their own destruction—from him and from Zeus, the god of hospitality. (In later years, whenever a relative of the dead suitors accosted him to ask for what they thought was justice, he found that these scenes had been stored away in his memory for instant recall.)

The suitors had a protégé of sorts, an emaciated, wrinkled old fellow named Iris who hung about the palace, living on leftovers and handouts. This Iris, naturally enough, had to challenge the new beggar—Odysseus recognized it as a turf war. But the suitors could not let it alone; they had to get involved, for the sadism of it, for the joke of it. They herded the two out of the banquet room, out through the entry gate, laughing at the prospect of watching old and decrepit men flailing at each other. It was a surprise to the crowd that had gathered to watch the sport when the newcomer demonstrated some rather sizable muscles when he had removed his raggedy old chiton and stood there in his loincloth, ready for the match. Telemachus said later that he had caught looks of nervousness and fear when the stranger solidly trounced poor Iris, who took a direct hit on the jaw, causing him to spew out a mouthful of broken teeth.

The boxing match was reported to Penelope, who rebuked her son for the treatment of the stranger in their halls. She had already learned of the beggar from Eumaeus. It was her habit to speak with strangers, a habit founded evidently on the hope that one of them would have direct experience of her long missing husband. Eumaeus warned her that even though this stranger maintained he had known Odysseus, every vagabond tended to make the same claim. Nonetheless, she had asked him to come to her quarters, an appointment that he, sensibly enough, suggested postponing until evening, when they might converse more in private. This response startled her; she was not used to inferiors determining the schedule. As she said later, her curiosity provoked her into making one of her rare appearances on the ground floor of the palace, where the suitors were as usual lounging about, waiting for an evening of roistering.

Odysseus watched the wife he had not seen for years descend the staircase, preceded by two women, her face obscured by a gauze-like veil. The room was dark where she entered; what light there was came from the fireplace, and it reflected a glow from her forehead and made a sparkle in the small pieces of gold that were suspended from her earlobes and shone out on the bracelets of her arm. The men grew silent at they perceived her progress across the room from the stair to one of the pillars that supported the great cross beams of the banquet hall. Odysseus watched her walk; twenty years had gone by, but she had not lost the precise movement in her step nor the characteristic slight forward thrust of her pelvis coupled with the stern, straight upright position of her back—a walk that would be likened in our own age to that of a runway model. There was so much that was deliberate about her now, he noticed; where once she had seemed so tentative, now she had become regal, he supposed one would call it, thinking back to Queen Arete on Scheria or to Hecuba, the old Trojan queen. He stared at Penelope's movements, reading their familiarity with uneasiness. It suddenly struck him then—hard, almost shocking him into breathlessness—that Penelope was a flesh-and-blood person whom he would soon encounter. (This was something he always mentioned later when he described this scene.)

She took up a position at the column, flanked by her attendants, her face still obscured by the veil which she clearly had no intention of lowering. Without moving her head in his direction, she launched into Telemachus angrily, how he had more sense as a child than as an adult, that from the look of him, handsome and prosperous, one would think that he came from the kind of background where people knew how to shelter strangers. She paused for breath, shifted her position to face him while the suitors shuffled uncertainly in place, and continued her tirade: how it was a shame and an outrage, that the entire island must know of his scandalous behavior. She then observed that Odysseus told her when her son reached his majority she should turn over the household to him, and prepare to remarry. Now was the time, she claimed, and the suitors should woo her properly, bringing gifts of cattle and other provisions rather than eating the food of another man's house.

Antinous replied sharply to this with the declaration that neither he nor any other of the suitors would budge until she chose one of them in marriage, and with that he turned to face them all, encouraging them to send their servants to their estates or wherever they were staying at the moment to bring Penelope appropriate courting gifts. Several suitors had their men out the door in a flash, and most returned within the hour. So it was that Penelope's female servants set off with her once again to mount the stairs, this time their arms loaded with a casket filled with precious jewels, the new round of gifts in what the suitors clearly thought was the final count-down to the gorgeous lady's remarriage. Odysseus laughed to himself at the time and, whenever in later years he thought of the magnifi-cent pieces of jewelry she brought in that evening, he laughed again.

Odysseus had the chance to see the anarchy of the palace that evening after Penelope had returned to her quarters. The suitors wished to dance, and a group of the young serving women stayed behind with them, ostensibly to keep the fires that provided illumi-nation. This was a chance for Odysseus to test them. In his disguise, he offered to mind the fires so that they could ascend the stairs to stay with Penelope among the other women. They began to laugh and jeer when Melantho—clearly their leader, brighter, better look-ing, more forceful—shouted out abuse, telling the old fool to mind his own business, that they liked it downstairs. The beggar's dark glare, his growl that he would tell Telemachus, and that she and the rest of the sluts would be cut into pieces, frightened the women somehow—maybe it was their guilty conscience, Odysseus used to say when telling the anecdote—and they fled back upstairs. The suitors had only one another to dance with that evening, and they were soon so drunk that they were falling over each other's feet when trying the intricate movements that the music indicated. This led to colliding bodies and quarrels, until suddenly the voice of Telemachus cut through the shouts, sharply ordering them out of the palace. The authority in his voice was as much a shock to them as a delight to Odysseus; he knew he had another solid ally for the showdown.

Penelope's surprise announcement that she was ready to

rewed had raised the ante, intensifying the pressure on Odysseus. The immediate next step was to prepare the banquet room where Odysseus envisioned penning the suitors in for the final slaughter. That very night, Odysseus told Telemachus it was time to remove the armor from the walls there. Eurycleia was summoned with the request that she keep the women upstairs while this was going on. They gave her as pretext that the smoke from the fireplace was dulling the metal, and it all should be put away for safekeeping.

Late that same evening Penelope came downstairs once again, this time to speak with the beggar. She lowered her veil and for the first time Odysseus could see the face of the woman he had married so long ago. The gentleness of the sweet smile of her youth was there, but drained of its merriment and replaced with a rueful acknowledgment of loss and pain. Her skin still stretched tight over her cheekbones and her eyes had deepened into her skull, as though it were no longer worth their while to contemplate what lay outside. Yearning for what is no longer there eventually makes the incomplete complete. Penelope, Odysseus was startled to observe, shared the empty stare of the captive women after the fall of Troy. It did not seem possible that she would come forth from the carapace of indifference that she had fashioned for herself.

In his disguise as beggar, he wove for her another fictional narrative, working in his encounter with Odysseus on the island of Crete. He had been blown off course on his way to Troy. The description of the encounter with Odysseus was painful to them both. Penelope silently cried at the memories the beggar was inspiring, while Odysseus was gripped with pain at the sorrow he had caused and now was impotently watching. They fell silent, each in the habit of endurance to which a lifetime of suffering had trained them. Then the beggar described with striking precision the pin that

Odysseus wore, which Penelope then exclaimed was the very one she had given him and pinned to his clothing as he left. The conversation went back and forth after that, she despairing of her husband's ever returning, he insisting that omens and sightings gave a forceful assurance that the man was within days of making an appearance on Ithaca.

Suddenly Penelope roused herself to call for maids to wash the beggar; the hospitality of the palace, earlier so shamefully neglected, would be extended, she said with a wry smile. The beggar demurred; no bath, he said, no girls, just a little wash, allowing that it would be enough if his dirty feet and legs could be cleaned. Penelope called on the old woman Eurycleia, who, it must be remembered, had nursed Odysseus as a boy. A large pan with water was brought out, and Odysseus' limbs were ready for the washing. Eurycleia forced a crisis upon Odysseus because of course she recognized the scar on his thigh made so long ago by the boar's lunging tusk. Quick thinking and luck—or was it Athena again?—averted catastrophe. He grabbed Eurycleia by the throat as she was about to emit a shriek of joy and secured her silence on his identity. All this time Penelope, who had risen from her seat and walked to the end of the room, stood apart. Could this be explained as a natural act of delicacy in one so refined, or had the goddess Athena sent a sudden impulse to her brain? Who will ever know? But Odysseus now had another important ally in Eurycleia.

Allies were of the essence, for events gathered even more momentum when Penelope returned to sit on her chair. As though she had been pondering the matter during her time apart, she declared that on the following day she would set up the contest of the bow and the axes. The bow was a mighty thing, the gift to

Odysseus from a certain Iphitus, whom he had befriended long ago, as the reader will recall, as a teenage ambassador from Ithaca to Messene. Whoever strung the bow, a task exceedingly difficult, well nigh impossible, and then sent an arrow straight through all the axes aligned in a row, that man would be her husband. One must wonder if Penelope had an intuition, formed by the exact description of the pin Odysseus wore, maybe by the sound of the beggar's voice, that somehow, somewhere her husband was indeed at hand, that the crisis of solution was now ready. How else can one account for the sudden decision to hold the contest, unless perhaps something within her finally gave way, and she surrendered the tension of her twenty-year resolve to fate?

The next day a banquet fit for the importance of the occasion was ordered. When he arrived with the beggar, Telemachus surprised everyone with the vehemence with which he reminded the suitors that he was the master of the house and would seat whom he chose at the meals.

Telemachus measured out the dirt floor in the great dining hall and dug holes to support the upright axes placed in a long line. Then he tried the bow, bending it substantially but not sufficiently to get the cord in place. Odysseus had given him a surreptitious negative nod when he seemed close to succeeding, so with a sigh the young man handed the bow back to Eumaeus, who proceeded to walk with it to the suitors. Each tried, each failed; only Antinous and Eurymachus, who had waited until the very last, remained to try their luck. At this point there was a break; no doubt they all had to piss, considering the tensions the occasion must have engendered. In any case, the old beggar while outside in the company of Eumaeus and Philoitius, the oxherd, drew the two of them aside, pulled up his clothes to reveal the scar on his thigh, and identified himself. They were quick to understand, and suddenly he had two more allies.

Back in the banqueting hall, after Antinous and Eurymachus had failed at their task, the old beggar spoke up, saying it was best to set the bow aside and wait until the next day when the gods would give them all more strength. But having said that, he then piously asked if he might try—just a silly request, he recognized—just to assess how much strength he still had in his tired old limbs. Their outrage was predictable. Antinous threatened him with every kind of viciousness if he were to persist in the idea. But Penelope insisted that he be given his chance. Telemachus spoke sharply to his mother, telling her that she had better retire to the women's quarters, that he was master of the banquet. Bite your tongue, mother! Odysseus, of course, could not have been more pleased; his son's smooth orchestration of Penelope's departure before he himself began the slaughter roused no suspicions.

As the last detail in his strategy, Odysseus told Eurycleia to throw the great bolt on the doors; he told her also to command her women to stay silent at their work, despite any cries they might hear coming from within.

Now the old codger got his chance. He bent the bow back easily, strung it, picked up an arrow, and, aiming unerringly, sent it through the axe holes. The men in the room froze in horror as he picked up another arrow, put it to the bow, cried out his name in ringing tones, then sent the arrow through Antinous' throat just as he was about to bring a goblet to his lips. In short order he had dispatched a dozen of them, weaponless as they were, and blocked from getting at him by Telemachus, Eumaeus, and Philoitius, and Athena in her disguise as Mentor. Then a crisis developed. The goatherd

Melanthius had somehow managed to climb in through a vent designed to evacuate the smoke of the room; he was intent upon sneaking weapons in to the suitors. But before the playing field could be leveled, Melanthius was stopped, trussed up by Eumaeus and Philoitius while Odysseus and his son with superhuman effort battled the suitors, until finally Athena, suddenly transforming herself into a bird, perched in the rafters and magically caused the spears cast by the suitors to miss their targets. Then, metamorphosing again, she began to wave her great shield, which caused the rest of the suitors to panic. Thus they were dispatched, all the suitors dead in a body, as they had clustered in life around the queen.

The banquet hall was spattered with blood and filth; it looked like an abattoir, dead bodies lying in heaps. Flies buzzed everywhere. When Eurycleia came in the room, she began to scream in joy, only to be silenced by her master, who claimed that exultation was out of place. These men had met the destiny, he said severely, to which they were all along heading because of their abusive and wicked behavior; the will of Zeus and the other gods had been visited on men who broke the basic law of society. With these words Odysseus seemed to be claiming that he himself, when he slew the suitors, was no more than the instrument of the gods. But in his punishment of the slaves he appeared as the author of vengeance. Melanthius, who had often spoken arrogantly to him when disguised as a beggar as well as allied himself with the suitors, was taken by Eumaeus, Philoitios, and Telemachus out on the porch. His hands and feet were cut off, as were his nose, ears, and genitals, and the body was thrown to the feral dogs for food.

Odysseus was also determined to avenge himself upon the serving women who had mocked him when he was in disguise, particularly the nasty Melantho. It is interesting from this distance to consider the situation of these women. Young girls were segregated into the women's quarters, a place for any women who might be unprotected, that is, without a male consort. As maximum protection, their quarters were above the ground floor; the only males with access to the area were boy children. But the female slaves were also required to serve the suitors their meals; they were downstairs, unprotected and at their mercy. Think of a contemporary rowdy bar scene with women trying to thread their way among the tables and the standing groups of weaving drunken males while serving the beer. It turned out that twelve of the female slaves began sexual relationships with the young men. It seems obvious from our perspective that the younger and sexier of the slave girls would have had no way to resist the advances of these roistering suitors, swollen with youthful desire, fired up as they were not only by alcohol, but by the fantasy of the powerful marriage they had the chance of making. We say "advances," and we think of a mix of heavy sweet talk, pressure, threats, physical gropings, the arrogance of aristocratic adolescents, and the acquiescence of slave women. The truth, pure and simple, is that these women must have been raped repeatedly by the men from the day of their arrival.

Yet when Odysseus had returned, killed the suitors, and reinstated himself as king, the women were to be punished. His old nursemaid, Eurycleia, was quick to point an accusing finger at those slaves among the fifty working in the household who, she claimed, had slept with the suitors. "They went down the path of shamelessness," she said. In a culture that put great store by shame, a woman who surrendered her virginity out of wedlock and was known to have done so was shameless—at least as Eurycleia understood the idea. But a slave, it must be noted, had no rights over her own body, and when she was among lustful young men, she no doubt considered it better to submit than to be battered and forced. Eurycleia said of the others that she had taught them all they knew. For this generality she used as her examples, curiously enough, "how to card wool" (which is to define them as a human mechanical contrivance, one may say), and "how to endure their slavery" (which would be something like denying their personhood so as to have the soul of a machine). One might guess that the old woman denounced these women, "these shameless creatures," as she would have called them, because in accepting their situation they wished to preserve their humanity as much as possible and so began something approximating concubinage; that is to say, they established themselves in a relationship instead of remaining a convenience, mere comfort women.

Odysseus, who was so often entirely rational and cool in his judgment of the suitors and their misbehavior, grew angry in response to Eurycleia's revelation. Of course, the night before he had had to put up with the high-handed manner of the slave woman Melantho, who was the mistress of Eurymachus, a principal among the suitors. He was inclined to store up this kind of thing. After Eurycleia's denunciation, slave-owning Odysseus determined to put the dozen slaves to the sword. Telemachus, however, devised a torture far more horrible by hanging them together in a giant noose, garroted with a slow, cruel death. Sadism for some can be very sweet revenge, indeed very erotic. One can imagine that the boy beginning when he was in his late teens, perpetually aroused, perpetually frustrated, had no doubt listened one time too many to the partying, thumping, and moans emanating from the banquet hall and throne room evening after evening. Now it was payback time. Odysseus, for his part, was probably thinking of the slave women ruining his property—their bodies—in their surrender to sexual intercourse. Their bodies, his property, damaged goods, penetrated and handled nightly, these images must have produced a rush of anxieties of all sorts in the male proprietor.

But let's pause a moment. There could be another interpretation of those moments now so long gone in time: that perhaps Eurycleia was right, that the twelve women were a nasty lot, well perhaps "disloyal" is the better word, which would definitely be "nasty" in Eurycleia's vocabulary. They had figured out that Odysseus was probably not coming back, that Penelope would have to marry one of these suitors. They had seen her any number of times on her promenades, they knew she was older than she let on. The man who married her, they considered, would be getting a queen and with her a throne, but not really much in the way of fun in bed. So they were solidifying their positions, each of them getting one of the suitors accustomed to her charms, so that when and if that man got the nod, she would come along with him. Not as his queen or consort, of course, but something like *maîtresse en titre*, if such a notion even crossed their minds in Ithaca. This explains what to some contemporary minds seems like Eurycleia's excessive moralizing and Odysseus' cold determination to punish. However, we will let the motive for Telemachus' savagery stand. If nothing else, it suggests another dark, terrible motive for Penelope's famous fidelity when the suitors crowded around, and that is a deep fear of her son, in the knowledge of his fierce, cruel sexual rage. From a more positive view, one could argue that the cruel slaying of the maids was a tribute to—indeed, a kind of gift for—Penelope, as testimony to or in appreciation of the long grueling years of fidelity, which allowed Odysseus' son and heir to gain the throne.

Before Odysseus visited his vengeance upon the faithless serving women, he first forced them to wash down the blood-smeared walls, mop up the gore, wash the furniture, and restore the great hall to its pristine condition. Then finally Odysseus washed up himself. He remembered only too well how he had stepped forth from his bath in the river at the beach into the presence of the teenage Nausicaa, radiant in beauty bestowed by Athena. Now, he felt himself once again made young and glamorous by the goddess, his skin grow taut, his stomach muscles tighten, his back straighten. His gaze sharpened, the muscles of his face lifted, his lips curved up ever so slightly into a look of amiability. He did not need a mirror to know what it was that he presented at that moment to the reluctant and dubious Penelope.

Biologists with a literary bent might call this long history a Spermiad, since the human spermatozoa are ejaculated in great numbers into a bath of fluid through which they swim to the waiting egg, not unlike Odysseus on his long wandering sea voyage honing in toward the waiting Penelope. The sperm that succeeds first in piercing the exterior membrane causes the egg to emit a chemical that kills all the other contestants in the act of fertilization—just the very story of Odysseus and the suitors, one might say. Others point out that Odysseus is Cinderella, helped by Athena, the fairy godmother, sneered at by the suitors, the wicked stepsisters, put to the test of trying on the shoe, or stringing the bow in this case, to receive as the prize his wife, Cinderella's Prince Charming. But Odysseus had yet to meet Prince Charming, so to speak. Now was his moment.

The one constant in Odysseus' life was always his need to control and his success at it. Manipulating others had brought him to where he now saw himself master once more of the political situation in Ithaca. He entered the room in which his wife dwelled. He faced the woman he had married over twenty years earlier, his presence triumphantly announced beforehand by the old nurse Eurycleia, in whom Penelope had every confidence. The meeting initially fell quite flat. Instead of the crescendo he had long envisioned, he was perplexed to see that the lady was dubious, hesitant, altogether reluctant to accept his protestations of faith and identity, despite the embarrassed entreaties of Eurycleia and Telemachus.

But this was in fact Penelope's masterstroke. As though rousing herself from a torpor, she turned to Eurycleia and instructed her to make up the marriage bed, indicating a large bed in the corner of the room. As though struck, Odysseus leaped forward, shouting, demanding to know what had happened to the bed he had made from the olive tree, in the room he had created for the two of them. He spit out a catalogue of details, of building the bed, of building the walls, of the frescoes on the wall, the hangings, the carpets—the words were tumbling over one another as he spoke, scarcely coherently, the bubbles forming in the corners of his mouth he was so agitated. How ironic that in his need to control, he lost it completely, and surrendered to Penelope all the proof she needed that this wild creature was indeed her husband of twenty years ago! She led him then down the stairs to the room he had described; kept empty and fresh these many years, faithfully tended by the serving women. Now it was waiting for them, and they withdrew to it. It is not recorded how they passed what was almost a honeymoon night, so long had been the separation, so ardent the yearning to be reunited. What is known is that they stayed up long beyond their customary hour for repose—no wonder! the events of the evening must have given them both an enormous adrenaline high—and they spent the time recounting their adventures and sufferings in the years of their separation.

The next day, it remained for Odysseus to proceed up the hill behind the palace to the farmland where his father had established himself some four years earlier. Eumaeus had described to him how Laertes, in his limited way, tried to maintain some regal identity, relating, for instance, the details of a sacrifice to which Laertes had invited all the old men whose sons were fighting at Troy. Eumaeus was there because he had to drive up the cattle that Laertes used in the ritual. The old men of Ithaca answered Laertes' invitation and, on the appointed day, trudged up the hill to his house set in the fields on a rise of land with an orchard some distance from the royal palace. Laertes, when he sighted them, came forward, greeted each with an embrace, and offered them places, seating them where the feast was about to take place. There were soft rugs of goat fleece set out on the grass in the shade of the trees. He gave them portions of meat taken from skewers that lay over the flames on metal andirons shaped like sailing vessels. Then he poured the wine for them into silver goblets that he had saved himself from the main palace when he moved up to the hills. They glittered in the sunlight, polished to perfection by his Sicilian woman.

"Let us pray to Poseidon, gentlemen, for this sacrifice is in his honor. All men need the gods." He held his goblet high. "Listen to our voices, Poseidon, you who encircle the earth, please grant what we seek from you in prayer. Be propitious to our sons who fight in far-off Troy, assure them a safe journey home; for you control the ocean and its waves."

On the day after his reunion with Penelope, as Odysseus made his way up the familiar path, he passed the tombs of his father's ancestors, two large chamber tombs, cut into a hillock that rose steeply in a clearing. He walked over to them, dismayed to notice that one had sustained damage in an earthquake; in the rubble he could make out bones, pots, long metal spits, and the boat-shaped andirons with which the wealthy and the royal males were customarily buried. It seemed so ignominious, but then, as he well knew, death betrays us all. Still, as he later told Telemachus, when he saw those tombs, he thought back to the funeral of Achilles at Troy, and wanted the same for himself. (It was a ritual of cremation, something that had not yet caught on in the distant provinces, Telemachus had explained defensively to the people of Ithaca when a decade later he had to plan the funeral of his father.)

Odysseus' first meeting with Laertes was a surprise to those who witnessed it, and somewhat of an enigma to the students of his life. Odysseus and his attendants went up into the hills to his father's farm, and found him dressed in rags as usual, looking a little vague the way old people can; of course, the stress of losing his wife and yearning for his lost son had clearly taken its toll. You could see it in his face, as everyone agreed. Odysseus stepped up to Laertes, did not embrace him, just stared at him. Laertes did not recognize him. Then Odysseus greeted Laertes as though he were a total stranger, told him one of those lies that he had told the suitors and everyone else down in the palace when he first came in disguised as a beggar. But, as his attendants said, it made sense down there. Now everything had been resolved, what was the point of doing it here? It was teasing, it was cruel, they were embarassed. Of course, a minute later he revealed himself, but there remains that curious fault in an otherwise seamless decorum. It was almost as though Odysseus had forgotten how to present himself except through a fiction. Or was he releasing a twenty-year-long resentment against his father? No one can say; neither man ever commented on it.

The first families of the territories forming the royal domain of the house of Laertes were in shock. More than six hundred young men, the prize of the land, had gone off to Troy at the behest of Odysseus and never returned. The promise of shiploads of Trojan plunder was an illusion. Their relatives now had to watch the cart-loads of valuables that Odysseus had brought back on the Phaeacean ship being drawn along the roads of Ithaca toward the storerooms of the palace. The parents of the suitors had ransacked their cupboards and chests, gambling their family heirlooms, jewels, elegant and costly objects of precious metals, woven stuffs, exquisite ceramic pieces, at the request of their sons who wished to compete success-fully in the contest for Penelope's hand. These young men were now all dead, unsuccessful in their quest, but their gifts were not about to be returned; instead they joined the other treasures cramming the shelves in the palace storerooms. The wealth of the land was gone into the palace; the flower of the land, the beautiful young men, had wilted and perished. These families were angry.

As expected, they marched on the palace in vast numbers. Odysseus faced one more crisis. It was shortly after he had gone to the hills to reunite with his old father; they were in fact at table enjoying one of those delightful Sicilian meals that Laertes' house-keeper habitually served, joined by some of the old man's faithful retainers, when news came of the gathering of angry men. Odysseus, Telemachus, and the farmhands once again prepared for battle, this time joined by Laertes, whose thrill at seeing his son had reanimated him sufficiently to want to join the fray. In the ensuing battle Athena intervened once more, bestowing upon the old-timer a last-minute makeover, and standing next to him, whispering encourage-ment, so that he managed to spear to death the equally aged father of Antinous. Then, having given the tottering old fellow his fifteen minutes of fame, she mounted aloft and shouted out to them all to cease.

In that arbitrary way, peace and stability came once again to Ithaca. In the end one would have to say that Odysseus succeeded in everything he did because Athena loved him, and his opponents had to understand that life was unfair. As a much later seer and prophet has said, many are called, few are chosen, and also to them that have shall be given, from them that have not shall be taken away.

Odysseus had himself put it very well in that eleventh-hour warning to Amphinomus which his son, Telemachus, memorized and carried in his heart: "Amphinomus, you seem like a fellow of sense, so I pray that you pay me heed. There are no living creatures more helpless than human beings, but when the going is good, they think they have the world by the tail, there is a bounce in their walk, heads held high, and they are not reckoning that then the bad times will come and they will suffer. It's all up to the gods, Amphinomus, so take what good things you get when you can, try to act with righteousness, because you never know, today you have what tomorrow you lose."

Odysseus had the intuition, it seems, to realize that the situation in Ithaca would heal itself faster if Telemachus were ruler in the palace and he were far away. In any case, when Odysseus had met Tiresias in the Underworld, the blind seer had prophesied to him that he would travel, and so he did. In subsequent years he was sighted now and again, just like Elizabeth, empress of Austria, another solitary traveler in a much later age. Penelope, however, remained at the palace, in the dowager apartments. As she told everyone, when Odysseus had related all the details of Tiresias' prophecy to her, she agreed that he must set forth. No doubt, for both of them, Odysseus and Penelope, the expectation of their great reunion was so magical, so pregnant, filled both of them with such deep feelings of yearning, loss, and desire that the actual nights spent in their nuptial bed were an impossible anticlimax. She preferred the company of her women, he preferred being alone on the road.

The record for both of them is incomplete after this point, and the various stories circulated about Penelope and Odysseus express the psychological needs of those who passed them on more than anything else. They are the stuff of gossip reporting which our more fortunate contemporaries may read in tabloids while waiting in the checkout lines of supermarkets. Those who needed to believe that justice must be served could take comfort in the story that the kinsfolk of the suitors brought Odysseus to trial (who knows under what jurisdiction?) and that Neoptolemus, Achilles' son, acting as judge (now there's a guy free of crime!), condemned him to exile. Those who wish to believe in the buddy system will be happy to know that he went into exile and later died in Aetolia at the court of King Thoas, his old colleague from Trojan War days. Those who never got over his forsaking the teenage Nausicaa will delight in the report that he married the young daughter of Thoas while in exile in Aetolia. Those who delight in his perpetual traveling and womanizing will be glad to know that he journeyed on to Epirus to live among the Thesprotians where he married Callidice, their queen, who bore him a son, Polypoetes. Those who, like Agamemnon, are convinced that a man can never trust his wife will be pleased to know that one account has it that Odysseus discovered evidence of Penelope's unfaithfulness, and either had her killed or drove her away from Ithaca. Those who need to believe that a woman cannot control herself when she is around a group of men will revel in the story that Penelope, claiming to have been seduced at the very end by the vicious Antinous (who, one will remember, she had declared more odious than all the rest), decamped to the Peloponnesus, where she gave birth to his son, the god called Pan. Those who believe that the Oedipal tendency tells all that there is to know about father-son and mother-son relationships will be pleased to learn that there circulated an epic poem in which Circe is said to have borne a son, named Telegonus ("Born Far Away"), who as a young man set out to find his father, and arriving on the shores of Ithaca met and killed an unknown assailant who wished to bar him from entering the land. It was of course his father, Odysseus, whose widow, Penelope, promptly took up with Telegonus, while Telemachus, clearly de trop in this domestic drama, sailed to Aiaia and bedded, if not wedded, Circe. It is a kind of *La Ronde* all of its own.

In reality, ten years after the great killing Odysseus slipped into town one night just as weary, dirty, and storm tossed as when he had presented himself in disguise to Eumaeus. The palace servants let him in finally after quite a tussle when he lifted his leg and showed them the scar on his thigh, and one or two of them remembered old Eurycleia, now dead, telling the story of Odysseus and the scar. Telemachus was summoned, and he was shocked to see how his father had deteriorated mentally. The old fellow knew his son, recognized the palace, but only every once in a while. He was sharp as a tack, however, when it came to telling the story of the Trojan War—although he could only seem to do it in a kind of poetic style, not at all in prose. Telemachus did not tell him that Penelope was dead, like his mother, Anticleia, from one of "the arrows of Artemis," the Bronze Age explanation of myocardial infarction.

Telemachus took his father in and installed him in spacious quarters near the throne room. His son lavished every attention on the old fellow—no want was left unsatisfied. Although Odysseus was no doubt too dim by this time to perceive the irony of it all, Tiresias' prediction did come true: Odysseus did, indeed, end his days "well-fed and pampered."

Within a year Odysseus himself was dead, completely gaga by this time. It was long past time for him to go; his teeth, so many of them fractured in battles long ago or damaged in his travels, were mere rotted stumps, if even that, giving him bouts of pain that drafts of wine only barely narcotized; both his eyes were dim from cataracts; the celebrated acuity of his hearing was altogether gone; his limbs ached from arthritis and were deformed from hairline cracks that had healed poorly. As he surveyed the earthly remains, Telemachus, who was so in love with his father's great heroic image—as a substitute for the love he might have felt for a father had he ever known him—determined to honor that request for an elaborate cremation made a decade earlier, and he prepared the funeral very much as his father had described that of Achilles when he died and was buried on the field at Troy. The old women of the palace bathed the body, anointed it with oil, dressed and adorned it with flowers, wreaths, ribbons, and jewelry. This was done on the first day of his death, and the body, displayed on a platform, remained among the women until the unmistakable smell of the beginnings of putrefaction made it clear that Odysseus was not comatose, but indeed dead. Their role up to this point besides dress- ing the body was to lament over Odysseus in a ritualized way, stylized keening learned by women one generation after another.

Telemachus had a pyre built one hundred feet square. He and his men laid the body at the top, and after skinning a quantity of fat sheep and cows, they wrapped Odysseus' corpse in the fat so as to kindle a gigantic blaze, placing the animal carcasses on all sides. Then two-handled jars of oil and honey were laid against the bier, four stallions were driven to the top and slaughtered, together with two dogs, ones the deceased king had said he favored in the brief time between the slaughter of the suitors and his subsequent depar- ture from home. The people of Ithaca had been gathering dead trees and fallen branches for days to make the stuff for a great blaze. It was possible to see the light of the flames over on Cephalonia as the fire burned for an entire day and night. When the fire cooled they collected the bones and placed them in a giant terra-cotta urn decorated with rows of warriors and their shields, horses, chariots, and a grand array of spears that formed bands encircling the piece. They then placed the urn in one of the two chamber tombs, both now restored to their traditional glory.

Such was the splendor of the cremation ceremony and the subsequent procession to the burial site that within a year the people of the area began to leave small offerings before the tomb, praying at the same time that the spirit of Odysseus would be propitious to whatever undertaking or desire they entertained. This was the beginning of his hero cult, which was transferred to a cave in the vicinity (there archeologists more than two millennia later uncovered twelfth- and eleventh-century B.C.E. cups and votive tripod-caldrons from the ninth century). On the mainland across from Ithaca, an Aetolian people, the Eurutanai, paid him heroic honors, consulting a shrine in his honor they had built for purposes of divination; they called it the oracle of Odysseus. Farther on in the Peloponnesus, in Laconia, Odysseus was worshiped as a hero purely because he was the husband of Penelope, who was born in those parts. On the coast of Libya, Greek-speaking people also established a ritual of worship to Odysseus in recognition of the fact that the territory was commonly thought to be the ancestral home of the Lotus-eaters.

At the time of the great killing, Phemius, the court singer, had been caught in the room with the suitors as the slaughter began. His outcries and protestations of loyalty were enough to get Telemachus to indicate to his father that the singer should be saved. Not long after, however, Phemius left Ithaca, his nerves too jangled by the entire experience. On the mainland, at another court where he was trying to establish himself, he met a colleague in the oral epic business, Demodocus was his name, who had made his way across the Mediterranean from the island of Scheria. One evening when the two men were comparing notes, they found that each had anecdotes of Odysseus in his repertory; Demodocus had paid close attention when Odysseus had entertained Alcinous and Arete with stories of his travels, and Phemius, of course, had lived through the whole nightmare at Ithaca ("The noise, my dear, the people!"). Lightning struck, and they decided to work together sharing their material on a master narrative poem, sort of like the *Iliad*. People, they noticed, were getting just a little tired of that one, and it was definitely time for something new. Odysseus would be the hero of their story, and they would call it the *Odyssey*.

What would a modern say about this man, if he were asked to give a stonecutter words for his epitaph?

Masking inward joy with outward cool, humble in his understanding of the powers that hold humankind, arrogant in his assumption of his own worth, sociable and personable toward every kind of person though never sympathetic, always private, sensual, and fastidious, cruel and cunning, serious and dignified, Odysseus is the superlative role model for males of the ancient world.

SOURCES

Odysseus is mentioned in many ancient texts, most prominently in the *Odyssey*. The world at large considers this poem and the *Iliad* to be the work of Homer. There is, however, no surviving manuscript of these poems until centuries after they were thought to have been composed. Contemporary theory has it that they date to a time when they must have originated as oral narratives, performed again and again in circumstances of which we know nothing, changed and improved over considerable time. Because there are substantial datable differences in context between the two poems, many scholars assume different authorship for the two works. These facts—if indeed, we may call them that—suggest that assigning the authorship of the two to a certain Homer, little more than a name attached to quaint anecdotes in ancient Greek literary history, is fine as a convenience, as long as no one believes that there is a genuine historical person behind the name. A work whose origins are clouded in such obscurity has naturally enough excited the interest and imagination of centuries of thinkers and scholars trying to work out its first beginnings and subsequent transmission. None of this is really important for the biography at hand, but for those who are inclined to want to know about such things, read my *Ancient Epic Poetry* (Cornell University Press, 1993) for an overview of the subject.

The other text, of course, that features Odysseus in some detail is the *Iliad*. Naturally I have taken liberties with both poems, using them often more as inspiration than as a line-by-line guide. For instance, in the *Odyssey* the presentation of Odysseus' seven years spent with Calypso is confined to a description of the garden around her cave, her anger at having to give Odysseus up, her offer of immortality, his declining it, and the scene of his departure, all of this material in the fifth book of the poem. A couple of times there occurs the one-line observation that he lay with her in bed each night, although unwillingly. I have conjured up the details of what must have been in some ways a tortured personal relationship over a span of seven years, and have attempted to fill out imaginatively what he and she must have been doing all day long and how it was that no ship ever came by to rescue him. These are the questions that a close and slow reading of these texts will inspire but that, in the original rapid-fire oral delivery of the poem, the auditor would have had no chance to pursue. An oral poet, like any stand-up, improvisational performer, can quite rightly get away with all sorts of things that a reflective reader might want to investigate.

I have also moved material around, as for instance when I bring in Odysseus' visit to his grandfather when he was wounded by the boar to the time of his adolescence; in the *Odyssey*, however, it constitutes a brief flashback digression late in his life, at the time when Eurycleia recognizes the scar on the beggar's leg. Likewise the story of Eumaeus' childhood, which he offers up as afterdinner entertainment to the wayfaring stranger some thirty or so years after the fact, I return to its natural chronological position as a childhood revelation made by the slave boy Eumaeus to young Odysseus and his sister. Both events serve aesthetic and narrative ends in the *Odyssey* text that have nothing to do with a reconstruction, however fictitious, of the life of Odysseus. Because Odysseus' declining years and death are never described, I have taken the descriptions of the funerals of Patroclus and Achilles from the *Iliad*, added details from Donna Kurtz and John Boardman's *Greek Burial Customs* (Thames & Hudson, 1971), and made a bang-up funeral for our hero.

The *Iliad* covers the war years at Troy, but I have used two other important sources for the so-called facts of his life for this period. These are two tragic dramas composed in the fifth-century B.C.E. by Sophocles. *Ajax* covers the events of the madness and suicide of its eponymous hero and the subsequent argument among the Achaean chieftains over his disgrace and burial, wherein Odysseus provides almost the only voice demanding that Ajax receive the respectful treatment that his years of glorious service to the army demand. The other, *Philoctetes*, relates the somewhat dubious behavior of Odysseus when he works out a scheme to trick the wounded hero into returning to Troy. In this latter play we can see the tendency of artists after the time of Homer to focus on Odysseus' capacity for inventing stories, transforming it into the ethical failing of blatant manipulative lying. The instinct to manipulate and control seems to me an interesting characteristic already fully alive in the Homeric Odysseus, and I have made much of it in this biography.

Other details—such as his recognizing Achilles at the court of Lycomedes, pretending to be crazy so he can avoid the draft, his plot against Palamedes, the stealing of the Palladium, the strategy of the wooden horse—were narrated in epic poems, gathered together into what is now called the Epic Cycle, the texts of which have not survived. We know of these bits and pieces only from Apollodorus (or, as most scholars believe, someone several centuries later who faked his style and name), who was one of those Alexandrian fact mavens who made a compendium of such historical details in two works entitled *Bibliotheke* and *Epitome*. Apollodorus, or whoever he is, is a very important source for details of the life of Odysseus. Euripides' *Iphigenia in Aulis* has a very brief mention of the morally dubious role Odysseus played in deceiving Clytemnestra in the matter of her daughter's killing, and there are the occasional references to Odysseus in the second-century B.C.E. Pausanias' *Description of Greece*, as one can determine from a glance at the index of names. Those who have access to the Internet may consult the website www.perseus.tufts.edu, which offers a cornucopia of information. Homer (whoever he, she, or they may happen to have been who wrote the *Iliad* and the *Odyssey*) assumes that his (her, their) audience already knows the contextualizing details; so few are given in the narrative.

Likewise, as scholarly theory posits, the narratives of the two poems took shape over several centuries during which time customs and physical contexts changed but were not always registered in the text. The most notorious is the description of bronze armor and iron farm utensils, which signals an orginal Bronze Age setting for the narratives carried over to an Iron Age audience. For that reason the text is unstable when it comes to "realistic" descriptions. Emily Vermeule, whose *Greece in the Bronze Age* (University of Chicago Press, 1964) remains one of the best descriptions of information available from archeological excavation for that period, resolutely refuses to consider evidence from the poems because she considers them such an unrealistic mélange (the same might also be said of the context which I have created for my fictitious hero). In her book one will find a judicious account of the details of palace architecture, clothing, jewelry, art, vase paintings—everything material from the late second millennium B.C.E. This can be supplemented with, for instance, *Ancient Greek Dress*, edited by Marie Johnson (Argonaut, 1964); Lionel Casson's *The Ancient Mariners* (2d ed., Princeton University Press, 1991); J. J. Coulton's *Ancient Greek Architects at Work* (Cornell University Press, 1977); J. K. Anderson's *Hunting in the Ancient World* (University of California Press, 1985); David W. Tandy's excellent *Warriors into Traders* (University of California Press, 1997); and perhaps most valuable of all, although dry as dust in its presentation, *A Companion to Homer*, edited by Alan Wace and Frank Stubbings (Macmillan, 1963). M. I. Finley's classic *World of Odysseus* has recently been republished (New York Review Classics, 2002), in which the celebrated ancient historian sets out to do exactly what Vermeule argues cannot be done.

I urge the reader to read and view the first hundred pages of John Camp and Beth Fisher's *The World of the Ancient Greeks* (Thames & Hudson, 2002), which offers splendid photographs of sites, vase remains, etc., from this early period. The page on Pylos is especially instructive—I have used the excavation of the palace there for my fictive reconstruction of the palace at Ithaca, for which no evidence exists.

The island of Ithaca itself is a disputed subject. I have arbitrarily agreed with those who identify the present-day island of Itháki with the ancient home of Odysseus—all of it being deliciously crazy in any case, because what is the point of trying to assign a true piece of real estate to a fictive character from a fictional narrative? Still, I strongly urge those who want to luxuriate in the settings of Ithaca and Troy to get J. V. Luce's *Celebrating Homer's*

Landscapes (Yale University Press, 1998), a truly exquisite book of photographs and descriptions of the fighting fields of what we may imagine to have been Troy and the island home of Odysseus.

Most of all, the reader will enjoy and profit from the original Homeric texts in their English translations. This has been done very handsomely for the present generation by Robert Fagles (Viking, 1996). Taped readings of Fagles' translation of the *Odyssey* have been made by Ian McKellen. Odysseus as a character who becomes an idea that changes and adapts over the millennia from culture to culture has been brilliantly described by W. B. Stanford in *The Ulysses Theme* (Blackwell, 1954).

GLOSSARY

Achaeans	Name for the people of Greece in the second millennium B.C.E.
Achilles	The principal warrior of the Achaeans
Aegisthus	Agamemnon's cousin, Clytemnestra's lover
Aeneas	Trojan prince, son of Anchises and Aphrodite
Aeolus	Supernatural being who controlled the winds
Agamemnon	King of Mycenae, leader of the Achaeans, husband of Clytemnestra
Aiaia	Island home of Circe
Ajax	A name of two Achaean warriors
Alcinous	King of the Phaeacians
Amphinomus	A principal suitor for Penelope's hand
Amphithea	Odysseus' maternal grandmother
Andromache	Hector's wife
Antenor	Prince of Troy, protected by Odysseus
Anticleia	Mother of Odysseus

Antilochus	Achaean warrior, Nestor's son
Antinous	A principal suitor for Penelope's hand
Aphrodite	Goddess of fertility and reproduction
Apollo	God of music and archery
Ares	God of war
Arete	Queen of the Phaeaceans
Arkeisios	Paternal grandfather of Odysseus
Artemis	Goddess of the hunt and of nature
Astyanax	Son of Hector
Athena	Odysseus' patron deity, goddess of intelligence and craft
Aulis	Harbor in northeast Greece where the Achaean fleet assembled
Autolycus	Odysseus' maternal grandfather
Briseis	Achilles' slave girl trophy
Calchas	Priest of Apollo attached to Achaean army
Calypso	Nymph on the island of Ogygia
Cassandra	Princess of Troy
Cephalonia	Island near Ithaca
Charybdis	A malign sea element that destroys ships
Circe	Witch who transforms men into swine
Clytemnestra	Wife of Agamemnon, sister of Helen
Ctimene	Odysseus' sister
Cyclops	A one-eyed giant
Dawn	The goddess who loved Tithonus, also known as Eos
Demeter	Goddess of agricultural fertility
Demodocus	Singer at the court of Alcinous and Arete
Diomedes	King of Tiryns, Odysseus' comrade in arms in the fighting
Echeneos	Courtier to King Alcinous

Elpenor	A member of Odysseus' crew on the voyage home
Eumaeus	Slave swineherd
Euryalus	Aristocratic Phaeacean youth
Eurycleia	Nurse to Odysseus, and then to Telemachus
Eurylochus	Odysseus' brother-in-law, companion
Eurymachus	A principal suitor for Penelope's hand
Hades	King of the dead in the Underworld, also sometimes the name for the place
Hector	Prince of Troy, principal defender of the city
Hecuba	Wife of Priam, queen of Troy
Helen	Wife of Menelaus, sister of Clytemnestra
Helenus	Son of Priam, Trojan prince, priest
Helios	God of the Sun
Hephaestus	God of the forge, sometime husband of Aphrodite
Hera	Goddess, wife of Zeus
Hermes	God of boundaries, messengers, and thieves
Icarius	Father of Penelope
Idomeneus	King of Crete, Achaean warrior
Ionian Islands	Island group that includes Ithaca
Iphigenia	Daughter of Agamemnon
Iphitus	Prince in Messene, gave bow to Odysseus
Iris	A beggar hanging out at the palace in Ithaca
Ismaros	A town in Thrace
Ithaca	Island home of Odysseus
Laertes	Father of Odysseus, king of Ithaca
Laestrygonians	A people encountered by Odysseus
Laodamas	Son of Alcinous
Leda	Mother of Helen and Clytemnestra
Lemnos	Island where Philoctetes was left by the Achaean army

Lotus-eaters	A people encountered by Odysseus
Lycomedes	King at whose palace Achilles was hidden
Maleia	Cape at southeast corner of Peloponnesus
Melanthius	Goatherd at Ithaca loyal to the suitors
Melantho	Slave serving woman at Ithaca, mistress of Eurymachus
Menelaus	King of Sparta, husband of Helen
Mentor	A palace retainer left in charge at Ithaca
Meriones	A fellow warrior at Troy
Mycenae	Agamemnon's citadel
Mycenaeans	The people of Greece
Nausicaa	Daughter of Alcinous and Arete
Neoptolemus	Achilles' son by Dedameia
Nestor	Elderly ruler of Pylos, Achaean warrior
Ogygia	Island home of Calypso
Olympus	Mountain site of the palace of the gods
Palladium	A small statue of Athena, good luck piece at Troy
Paris	Prince of Troy, paramour of Helen
Parnassus	A mountain in Autolycus' homeland territory
Patroclus	Achilles' companion
Peisistratus	Son of Nestor, befriends Telemachus
Peleus	Husband of Thetis, father of Achilles
Peloponnesus	Name of Southwestern area of mainland Greece
Penelope	Wife of Odysseus
Phaeaceans	People inhabiting the island of Scheria
Phemius	Singer at the court in Ithaca
Philoctetes	Achaean warrior, kept from battle by a wound
Phoenix	Old friend of Achilles' family
Polyphemus	Name of the Cyclops Odysseus encountered, son of Poseidon

Poseidon	God of the sea, brother of Zeus
Priam	King of Troy
Proteus	A sea sprite, herder of seals
Pthia	Ancestral home of Achilles
Pylos	Locale of Nestor in southwestern Peloponnesus
Scamander	River on the plain of Troy
Scheria	Name of the island home of the Phaeaceans
Scylla	A malign riptide that sucks ships under
Scyros	Island home of Lycomedes
Simoïs	River on the plain of Troy
Sparta	City of the Peloponnesus, royal seat of Menelaus
Sthenelus	Diomedes' charioteer
Telemachus	Odysseus' son
Thetis	Mother of Achilles, wife of Peleus
Thrace	Land of northeast Greece
Thrinacia	An island where the Sun God kept his cattle
Tiresias	An Achaean seer and prophet
Tiryns	Site of a Mycenaean citadel near Mycenae, ruled by Diomedes
Tithonus	Human lover of Dawn, who was given immortality but continued to age
Trojans	People of Troy, enemies of the Achaeans
Tyndareus	King of Sparta, father of Clytemnestra
Zeus	Major male deity of the Greeks, husband of Hera